Windmills

PIERCEHAVEN BOOK 2

ROBIN MERRILL

New Creation Publishing

New Creation Publishing
Madison, Maine

Chapter 1

When the Piercehaven girls' basketball team returned to school on Monday morning, they were ushered into the gym, where they were lauded and applauded ad nauseam before the rest of the student body.

Emily stood leaning against the wall pads on one end of the gym, watching the spectacle. Dominic Hill, the small high school's only math teacher, who was, like Emily, enduring his first year teaching at Piercehaven, stood beside her, his arms folded across his chest.

"Is this ever going to end?" Emily muttered to him.

His eyes widened. "Didn't you coach them to this coveted state championship? Shouldn't you be out there prancing around with the rest of them?"

"Nah, I wasn't really a coach. I just sort of hung around there toward the end."

Dominic nodded. He knew what she meant—near the end of the season, the girls' basketball coach had been arrested for sexually assaulting his players. Emily's sort-of-fiancé had taken over the coaching position, and Emily had helped with the emotional fallout.

"Besides," Emily continued, "this is only your first basketball season here. Isn't it a bit early for you to be so sour?"

"Maybe," he admitted, "but I came into work today happy that basketball was over. Then first thing I know, we're all herded in here for another pep rally. Isn't enough enough?"

"This will probably be the last hoorah," Emily tried to encourage him. "Until next season, anyway."

"Well, I won't be around for that."

It was her turn to look surprised. "Really?"

"Yep. Don't go spreading that around, but of course I won't be here. I'm betting if you hadn't hooked up with a lobsterman, you'd be out of here too."

This statement annoyed her immensely, but she tried not to let it show.

"Just look at them," he said. "The girls' team is on the floor celebrating. The boys' team is in the bleachers, looking jealous. And every single other student looks absolutely miserable. Look at Sara Crockett!"

Emily looked. Sara's clothes were black. Her generous eyeliner was very black. Hair, black. Boots, black. "She always looks like that," Emily said.

"Look at her facial expression right now, though. She would rather be anywhere but here."

"I know, I know. You're right."

"Look at DeAnna!"

Emily looked. DeAnna Anderson sat isolated, on the edge of the second bleacher. Her shoulders were slumped, her eyes red. "Has she been crying?" Emily wondered aloud.

"I don't know, but probably. That kid has a rough life."

"So then let's not blame her tears on the girls' basketball team."

"You're starting to sound like you do belong here, Miss Morse. No, from what I hear, that kid's got plenty to be miserable about, but still, this isn't helping. I think *I'm* sick of the basketball hoopla? What about her? How sick of it is she?"

Emily snickered.

"What?" He looked at her.

"You said *hoopla*."

"So?"

"So? You said *basketball hoopla*."

He grimaced. "I hate puns."

"Sorry. I love them. And you're absolutely right. Half the kids in this school don't play basketball, and we don't give them any other options."

"There's baseball," he said.

"But there's no softball. How ridiculous is that?"

"There's cross-country."

"And how many kids run cross-country?" she asked.

He laughed. "I don't remember. Four?"

"Exactly."

"Well, we should have a softball team."

"We should," she agreed.

He was staring at her.

"What?"

"No one else is going to do it."

"Oh yeah? Well, then why don't *you* do it?" she asked.

"I've already applied for about ten jobs, and half of them start immediately. I can't get out of here fast enough."

Principal Hogan dismissed the assembly, and Mr. Hill vanished, but Emily stood where she was, watching Sara climb out of the bleachers, her face expressionless. Her T-shirt said, "I love to hate things."

DeAnna was the last student to stand up, and when she did, she left a ten-foot buffer between herself and the rest of the student body as they slowly filed out of the gym.

Emily felt a little guilty for not doing a better job of reaching out to DeAnna, but DeAnna wasn't an easy kid. She was argumentative, rude, and just generally unpleasant. *How much Jesus must love that child*, Emily thought, and vowed to do a better job of following his lead.

Chapter 2

On Tuesday morning, junior Thomas and sophomore Chloe were waiting in Emily's classroom when she got there. They sat side by side, facing Emily's desk, as if waiting for a meeting with a loan officer. Emily plunked her giant purse down on her desk. "Morning, guys."

"Are you going to the meeting tonight, Miss Morse?" Chloe asked.

Emily felt a small panic. "What meeting?" she asked, trying not to show her alarm.

"The co-op meeting," Chloe said.

Emily noticed Thomas was being unusually reticent.

"Why would I go to a lobster co-op meeting?" Emily asked.

"Not the lobster co-op—the *power* co-op," Chloe said.

For a second, Emily still didn't know what she meant. Then it dawned on her. "Oh, the electric company? Why are people going to an electric company meeting?"

Thomas looked up at her. "Are you serious?"

"What?" Emily's eyes flitted between the two young, earnest faces. "What am I missing?"

Chloe didn't seem surprised by Emily's cluelessness. "They're going to vote on the windmills."

Emily started to ask, "What windmills?" but Thomas cut her off before she could.

"They're not going to *vote* tonight. They're just going to talk about it."

"They've been *talking* about it since I was eight! Isn't it time they make a decision?"

Thomas shrugged and looked down at Emily's desk.

"Well," Chloe continued, "my mom said they're actually going to vote, now that the whole thing is possible."

Emily wanted to ask what new circumstance made the "whole thing" possible, but Thomas cut her off again.

"So how are the wedding plans coming?" he asked.

She gave him a smirk. "You'll be the first to know." She didn't know how Thomas knew about her sort-of-engagement, but he wasn't the only one.

James hadn't really proposed yet. He had just promised that he *would* propose. And she had promised to accept. But she didn't think this counted as a real engagement. Still, several people had already asked her when was the date, would the wedding be on the island, did she need any help. This all meant, of course, that James had told someone something. She hadn't told a soul—not even her mother. She was too scared the whole thing wouldn't happen and she'd end up looking the fool.

"Be patient, Thomas! She doesn't even have a ring yet!" Chloe said.

"Well, there's not a lot of jewelry stores on the island. The guy's got to get to the mainland for a diamond. So why don't *you* be patient, Chloe?"

"You know you guys bicker like a married couple, right?" Emily said. Chloe blushed and looked down and Emily regretted her quip. "So where is the windmill meeting?" she asked, trying to cover her faux pas.

"At the church," Chloe said.

"You mean the *real* church?" Emily joked. She and Chloe were part of a small congregation that met for house church in their friend's basement, and people loved to ask them why they didn't just go to the "real church."

Chloe smiled, definitely getting Emily's joke. "Yes. That one. I don't think we'd all fit in Abe's basement."

"How many people do you think will come?" Emily asked.

"Well, if we're not going to vote, maybe only a hundred or so?" Chloe guessed.

Emily's eyebrows went up. She wasn't expecting such a high estimate.

"But if we *are* going to vote," Chloe continued, "and I think people think that we are, then well, I think we'll see, I don't know … everybody."

Thomas groaned, and Emily started to ask him why a windmill-meeting was groan-worthy, but the bell rang.

"Have a great day, guys."

"You too," Thomas said, and held out his hand for a fist bump, but it lacked its usual vigor.

Emily's first period freshmen filed in, and she opened her laptop so she could put the writing prompt up on the interactive board. She had planned to use, "If you had to erase one color from the world, what would it be and why?" But instead she typed, "Should

Piercehaven put up windmills?" Before she'd even typed the question mark, Tyler groaned.

"Are you serious, Miss M? We talked this to death yesterday in science."

"Good!" Emily said. "Then you should be able to easily organize your thoughts into a paragraph."

Tyler shook his head in disgust, but he did bend over his keyboard and look at the screen. Emily gave them five minutes to free write, and then, when she saw a few of them had gotten distracted, asked, "Would anyone like to share what they wrote?"

"You might not want to do that, Miss M," Tyler warned melodramatically.

"Why's that?" Emily asked, even though she had a pretty good idea.

"Because islanders are pretty passionate about their wind," Tyler said. "And their birds," he added, and several students laughed.

"Birds?" Emily asked.

Tyler leaned back in his chair, seeming to glow with the attention. "Yeah, birds. I never heard my grandmother even mention a bird, but now there's talk about windmills, and she's all, 'But what about the biiiiirds?'"

The class laughed again. Tyler looked quite pleased with himself.

"As in, the windmills will hurt the birds?" Emily said.

"Well, look at it this way," Tyler said. "A bird is only going to smash into a windmill once."

More laughter.

"OK, why don't you read what you wrote," Emily said to Tyler.

Tyler cleared his throat and read, "I don't care if this island gets windmills. I don't have to pay the electric bills, and when I'm eighteen, I'm leaving this stupid rock and I'll go live somewhere with cheap power." He looked up.

"That's it?" Emily asked.

"I'm a slow writer."

"OK then, thanks for sharing. Would anyone else like to share what they wrote?"

Victoria raised her hand.

Emily nodded at her.

She began, "My parents love the idea of windmills. They've been wanting windmills for this island since Vinalhaven put theirs up. It will save us money and it will save the environment—"

"Except for the birds," Tyler interjected.

Emily gave him a stern look and he shushed.

"People on this island are just scared of change," Victoria continued. "Once we put the windmills up, everybody will get used to it. Then it will be a good thing."

"Very good, Victoria. Anyone else?"

Sydney raised her hand. Then she began to read, "I have cousins on Vinalhaven—"

"No you don't," Tyler said.

"Shut up, Tyler!" Sydney snapped.

"Guys, we're not going to do this again," Emily said. "Tyler, behave. Sydney, continue."

"Third cousins twice removed," Tyler muttered, and the boys on either side of him laughed.

"As I was saying," Sydney continued, "my cousins say that they *haven't* saved any money on electricity since the windmills went up. And they also have migraines now, which are caused by the windmills. My dad says it is never going to happen for Piercehaven, because we are smarter than Vinalhaven. Besides, the windmills are *wicked* loud." She stopped reading and looked up at Emily.

"Migraines?" Emily asked, trying to hide her skepticism.

"For real," Caleb spoke up. "They say they cause all kinds of junk—puking, can't sleep, can't see, heart attacks."

Tyler swore to express his skepticism.

"Tyler!" Emily said more harshly. "Seriously! That's enough!" Then she looked at Sydney. "How loud can a windmill be?"

"You can hear it from more than a mile away," Caleb said. "I can hear Vinalhaven's from my boat in the morning when I'm fishing."

"But this island is only six miles long," Emily thought aloud. "Where can we put a windmill that's more than a mile away from everybody?"

"We can't," Caleb said. "That's the point. They want to put it on Chicken Hill, because that's the highest point. And yeah, not a ton of people live out there, but enough do."

"The poor ones," Tyler said. "The poor people live out there."

Chapter 3

When Emily got home, she used her ancient landline phone to call James. Cell phones didn't work on the island. As she dialed, she thought it a bit ironic that they'd be getting a windmill before a cell phone tower.

He answered on the second ring, surprising her. "I figured I'd have to leave you a message," she said.

"Nope. Caught me on the way to the fridge. What's up?"

"Don't suppose you're going to the windmill meeting today?"

"I wasn't going to. Why?"

"I don't know. I was just curious about the whole thing. Besides, it might be fun to see the inside of the 'real church.'"

"Are you saying you want to go?"

"I don't want to go alone."

"So are you saying you want *me* to go?"

"Oh, would you?"

He laughed and the sound of it made her stomach flip. "Sure. What time is it at?"

"No idea."

"OK, I'll find out. Want to grab a bite before?"

"Sure."

"Great. See you in a little bit."

He picked her up less than an hour later and took her to their usual haunt: The Big Dipper. The Big Dipper was actually a bar, one of only two on the island, but it served scrumptious pub food. Emily wasn't much of a cook, so she took every opportunity to dine at the Dip.

James ordered his usual medium-rare steak, but Emily got excited when she saw the special: lobster stew with a giant blueberry muffin.

She wasn't disappointed as she slurped up the buttery cream. "So," she said between mouthfuls, "you don't care about the windmills?"

James shrugged. "Not really. I don't know much about them. I mean, if they're going to save me a ton of money on electricity, then sure. But if they're going to torture the people who live near them, then maybe not. I'm not sure how the scale actually tips. People are still fighting over the windmills on Vinalhaven, and those have been up for years."

"How do we get our power now?" she asked.

He raised an eyebrow. "You don't know?"

"I've never had cause to wonder."

"It's an underground cable."

"That's a long cable."

"A-yuh. It sure is. And it's an expensive power supply. But, it's what we've got. That's why you won't see a lot of islanders heating their homes with space heaters."

"They say we'll be able to store the extra power from the windmills in thermal storage heaters."

He raised the same handsome eyebrow. "You been doing some research?"

"I did some Googling during my prep. Don't tell the taxpayers."

He wiped his mouth with his napkin. "I don't know, Emily. I guess if I had to choose, I'd vote nay. Maybe we should err on the side of caution. But, maybe we'll know more after the meeting."

The church was packed. Emily was reminded of the day of the state championship game, when nearly the whole island had stood at the ferry terminal cheering as the girls' basketball team boarded the boat. She'd thought then, "A lot of people live on this island." She thought the same thing now, except that now, people didn't look happy. Nary a pom-pom in sight.

A long table had been set up just in front of the altar. Four men and a woman sat on one side of it, looking anxious. Twenty rows of well-worn pews faced the panel, and someone had placed copious amounts of metal folding chairs in every available spot not taken up by pews.

The pews were filling up fast. The island's population was about a thousand. Emily looked around the sanctuary and was certain a thousand people couldn't fit. But from the look of the pushing match at the door, they were going to try.

A man in a WABI vest stood near a tripod in the corner, peering into a large camera. He was wearing headphones and looked like a hunter stalking his prey.

As Emily stared at the cameraman, Chloe slid into the pew beside her.

"I thought you weren't coming?" Chloe said.

"Did I say that? Well, you intrigued me. Is Thomas here?"

"No. He acts like he doesn't care, but I think the whole thing scares him."

"Scares him? Why?"

"Because, Miss M, they're going to put the windmills on *his* land."

"*His* land?"

"Well, yeah, his grandma's land, or I guess it's his dad's now that she died."

"His grandma died? The one who goes to this church?"

Chloe nodded.

"How did I not know about that?"

Chloe shrugged. "It *just* happened. There's been a lot going on."

One of the panel members stood, the scraping sound of his chair against the wooden floor serving to call the meeting to order. He cleared his throat. "Thank you all for coming. There seems to be some confusion about the purpose of this evening's meeting. Some of you have come prepared to vote, and some of you just to hear the facts about the issue." He cleared his throat again. Then he reached for a glass of water, picked it up, and then put it down again without drinking any of it. He continued, "But the board here hopes that, once you hear the facts, that you'll be able to vote tonight—"

"You can't call for a vote without announcing the vote beforehand," a woman called out from a pew near the back.

Emily craned her neck around to look at the woman and recognized her immediately. She was Duke and Sara Crockett's mother, Jane Crockett. Emily knew her from parent-teacher conferences. Tonight, her long dreadlocks were tied up in a colorful scarf, and she wore an oversized shawl that Emily figured she'd probably knitted herself. There was fire in her eyes.

"I understand that, Jane—" the man behind the table started.

"No, I don't think you do," Jane cried. "You're trying to do a sneaky vote, without inviting the people who actually have a stake in this thing!"

Various people around the room cried out "yeah!" in support of Jane's claim.

"We're not trying to be sneaky about anything ..."

Emily leaned toward James. "Who is this guy?"

"Darren McCormick, the co-op president."

Chloe must have heard them, because she added, "The guy to his left is Bobby Snyder, the Vice President. And the guy to his right is Oscar Pride. I don't know what his job is. Then the man on the end, that's Thomas's father. He's the treasurer."

"Yes, I recognize him. Remind me of his name?"

"Travis Payne."

"And the woman?" Emily whispered.

"Mabel Pride, Oscar's wife. I don't know what her job is either. I think she might be the secretary. She's also the one who actually works in the co-op office, you know, taking people's money and everything."

As Emily was getting the scoop on the board, the argument over whether or not to vote had escalated, until Duke hollered out, "Maybe we should vote on whether or not to vote."

Many laughed at this, and Emily felt a little proud of her **senior wisenheimer**.

The crack cleared the air. President Darren said, "I know some of you have concerns about putting up the wind turbines, and the board would like to address your concerns. Would anyone like to share his or her specific worry?"

Emily waited for Tyler's grandmother to call out, "The birds!" The thought even made her smile, and Chloe gave her a quizzical look. Emily tried to look stoic.

Darren called on Jane again.

"Where do I begin?" she said melodramatically.

Darren looked annoyed.

She continued, "First of all, this island, this beautiful island, our home, how are we going to mar its face"—her voice cracked as if she was about to cry.

"Never mind that!" Another man stood up. He wore a red and black plaid hat. "What about the money? You keep saying this is going to save us so much money—"

"Excuse me, Sam, but I was speaking!" Jane looked indignant.

But Sam continued to talk, raising his voice to drown her out, "—but how are we going to *pay* for the windmills? Last I heard those things don't just grow out of the ground!"

Darren held up both hands. "Let's address one concern at a time. Wind power *will* save us money. We've obtained an energy grant that will cover most of the purchase and installment. The rest will be covered by consumers—"

"Consumers?" Sam shouted. "Isn't that a fancy word that just means us?" He held out both hands to the crowd, who murmured their agreement.

"But," Darren continued, "you're going to be saving so much money by *not* piping in electricity from the mainland, you won't even notice the money you're investing in our future."

Sam guffawed derisively. "Don't try to talk circles around us, Darren. We're not stupid. And we haven't even talked about property value! The value of my property is going to tank when my ocean view is blocked by two giant ugly windmills."

"Oh, shut up, Sam!" someone called from the back. "You're never going to sell—you're fifth generation!"

"I can assure you," Darren calmly said from the front. "Your property value will not depreciate because of the windmills. That is simply not true."

Emily leaned toward James again. "What does Darren do in real life?"

"Real life?" James repeated.

"Does he make a living running this co-op?"

"Oh, no. He's a lawyer."

She stifled a giggle. "We have a lawyer on the island?"

"Well, he does mostly wills and real estate stuff. He's no Matlock."

"Matlock?" Emily said, failing to suppress the giggle this time.

"What? I grew up in the nineties. And we only had one channel."

Darren had given up on Sam and had moved on to Jane's concerns, which were plentiful. She didn't want to disrupt the fragile ecosystem of Piercehaven. She was worried about the animals, and she did mention birds, but she was also worried about the health of the island's human citizens. Jane said that the "infrasound" from the windmills caused a whole host of health problems, like insomnia, nausea, anxiety, allergies—

she even claimed infrasound caused nervous breakdowns and brain tumors. Emily looked around the room to see if the crowd seemed to be buying into any of this, and most of them did not.

As Darren tried to redirect her, another woman said, from somewhere near the front, "And now that we've heard from our resident conspiracy theorist, can we move on?"

Jane apparently had hawk ears because her eyes locked onto the back of the speaker's head. "Call me what you want. There's a well-documented case of a scientist actually thinking he saw a *ghost* because of the way this infrasound messed with his brain. Is that what we want?" She looked around the sanctuary dramatically. "Is that what you all want? To be tricked into seeing things that aren't even there? I'm telling you! We don't want to fill our island with noise, especially noise that we don't even understand!"

"OK," Darren broke in. "Thank you, Jane, but let's give someone else a chance to talk."

But she didn't sit down. "You said you were going to address my concerns. Well, are you?"

Darren took a deep breath and put his hands on his hips. "Only to say that there is no scientific data to support your claims. Vinalhaven has had wind turbines for years, and there have been absolutely zero reports of ill health effects. In fact, no one anywhere in the world has any health problems that can be tied directly to wind power."

Jane swore and sat down, still mumbling, "Just because we haven't heard about them doesn't mean they don't exist ..."

Someone else called out, "I don't want to hear any more about Vinalhaven. We are *not* Vinalhaven—"

"That is true," Darren said. "But we can still learn from them. Not only do they save money every month, but they are actually making money from tourists coming to see the turbines!"

James groaned. "Wrong thing to say, Darren."

"Tourists?" someone from the back screeched. "We don't want tourists! That alone is reason to vote no!"

The fight went on, with people essentially saying the same thing over and over. Darren continued to compare Piercehaven to Vinalhaven, which only further exacerbated the conflict. Emily couldn't understand why he didn't drop that particular angle.

Thomas's stepmom, Abby, stood and turned to face the majority of the crowd. "There are so many reasons to do this. We islanders don't like change, but some change is good. This will save us money. This will make us less dependent on the mainland. We will lose power less often. Please just try to see the positive and stop giving the knee-jerk rejection we do so well here. Let's stop trying to live in the past." She sat down.

At first, no one even acknowledged her little speech, but then a man called out, "And just how much money are you going to get for your dead mother-in-law's land?"

"Bojack!" Darren scolded. "Let's keep this civil!"

"No, I'd like to know that too," Jane said. "How much is the Payne family going to charge for this little parcel of land, which they're selling for the island's greater good?"

Jane's voice grew more sarcastic with each word.

"We're not buying anything," Darren said. "We've worked out a lease agreement." This announcement caused a small uproar.

The man named Bojack hollered over the din, "So we've got to give the Paynes money every single year? Sounds like a good deal for them. Not such a good deal for the people who actually live on that land."

"You don't live on that land!" someone in a green barn coat hollered.

"Close enough!" Bojack said. Then he swore at the barn coat wearer. "The Paynes sure don't. They're all cozy on the waterfront, now aren't they?" He looked at Thomas's father. "Your mother never would have done this, Travis. You should be ashamed."

Several people began to scold Bojack for crossing some sort of line, but he didn't seem to notice. Even more people were egging him on.

"Enough!" Darren shouted. "This is ridiculous. We're not getting anything accomplished. How about we all go home and cool off. Do your research. Have your discussions. We'll come back here on Thursday, and on Thursday, we vote. No matter what."

Chapter 4

Emily went into school early the next morning. She was concerned for Thomas and wanted to spend a little more time with him than she did on most mornings.

She beat Thomas and Chloe there. She flicked on the lights and crossed the room to her desk. As she settled in, Kyle, the social studies teacher, appeared in the doorway.

"Morning, Kyle," she said, trying to sound amicable. She wasn't Kyle's biggest fan. He'd proven to be a fair-weather friend.

"Saw you at the meeting last night," he said, keeping his distance.

"Oh? Sorry, I didn't see you there."

"No need to apologize. There were a lot of people there. I was just going to offer you some friendly advice."

"Oh yeah?"

"Yeah. Take it or leave it, but I just wanted to say, no matter where you fall on this thing, stay out of it. And it's probably going to be impossible to stay neutral. So you just might want to avoid the topic altogether."

She stared at him, processing what he'd just said. "Are you telling me I shouldn't have gone to that meeting?"

"No, of course not. I just … Emily, I do care about what happens to you. I want us to be friends. And while I know that you haven't taken my advice in the past, I hope you will believe me that this is going to get pretty heated, and you don't want to get caught up in it. Trust me."

"Trust you," Emily repeated phlegmatically.

Thomas and Chloe appeared in the doorway together, just in time.

"Like I said, take it or leave it," Kyle said, and he was gone.

"What was that all about?" Thomas asked.

"Do you guys ride to school together?"

"Yes, thank God," Chloe said. "I hate the bus. It smells like hot feet. Thomas is nice enough to give me a ride."

"That is kind of you, Thomas." Emily got up and shut the door. The two kids looked at her inquisitively. She didn't shut the door often. "Thomas, I was so sorry to hear about your grandmother. I would have said something earlier if I had known."

"It's OK," he said, even though it was clearly not OK. "Thanks."

"So tell me how you're really doing with all this windmill stuff."

He shrugged and looked down at his hands.

"Miss M!" Chloe chirped. "I heard you're starting a softball team!"

"What?" Emily was honestly shocked. "Where did you hear such a thing?" Then she had a thought. "Did you just try to change the subject on me?"

"It's OK, Chloe," Thomas said. "I'm all right, Miss M. I really don't care about it. I just wish it was over. I mean, it's going to happen. We've got the land, we've got the grant, and it's going to happen." He leaned closer to Emily. "Don't say this to anyone, but the wheels are already in motion. These few whiners who are bellyaching just need to shut up. It's not like we're putting up a nuclear plant or something."

"This is true," Emily said. "Are you getting flak about it? Or is your family?"

Thomas shrugged.

"Yes and yes," Chloe said. "But he'll be all right, Miss M." She put a hand on Thomas's back. "Thomas is tough stuff. And he has me to protect him." She raised her arm and flexed her bicep.

Thomas laughed at her, but his eyes remained serious. "A lot of island people already dislike my family because we're not dirt poor. This is no different. It will be all right."

"Remind me what your parents do for work?"

"My mom left the island, and us, years ago. But my dad is an accountant. And my stepmom helps him with that business. She's also a graphic designer. Works online, at home."

"I see."

There was a pause, and Chloe rushed to fill it. "But really, are we going to have a softball team?"

"Seriously, who *told* you that?"

"It's all over the school. Is it true? I'll play for you ... if it's true."

Emily looked at her. "Do you *want* to play softball?"

"I dunno. I've never played it before. But it sounds like fun."

"Do you think there would be any other interest?"

"I don't know. I could take a survey?"

Emily thought about that for a moment. Then the bell rang. "Sure," she said. "Take a survey."

No one mentioned softball during first period, but Emily's mind was busy mulling the idea over. Could she really do this? *Should* she really do this? She was surprised at the gut tickles the idea gave her. But she had been cooped up all winter, inside, on an island, and maybe she just wanted to get outside in the fresh air.

The bell rang and she traded in her freshmen for her juniors. As they settled in, she traveled around the room handing back papers. Hailey, their resident basketball superstar, asked, "Are we really going to have a softball team, Miss M?" "I don't know yet. Do you want to play?"

"I don't know," Hailey said slowly, but she looked intrigued.

Emily moved on to the next desk and handed an essay back to Hannah, who said, "I'll play!"

"Really?" Emily was surprised at her eagerness.

"Sure! Why not? I like to hit things."

Much of the class laughed at this admission as Emily stopped at the next desk. She looked down at DeAnna, who didn't look up at her. "How about you, DeAnna?"

Hailey gasped. Hannah's jaw dropped. DeAnna looked up, stupefied.

"What?" she asked.

"If we had a softball team, would you play?"

"I don't play sports."

Emily heard someone behind her snicker. DeAnna's cheeks got red, and she looked down at her desk. Emily regretted saying anything.

Noah came to the rescue. "It's never too late to start, DeAnna. Might be fun."

DeAnna didn't respond.

"Well, you don't have to decide right now. I still have to convince Mr. Hogan that we need a softball team. I don't even know if it's possible."

"Really?" Hannah said. "You're really going to try?"

Emily looked at DeAnna. "Yeah, I'm really going to try." Even as she spoke them, the words surprised her ears.

Chapter 5

A large ball of lead settled in Emily's stomach as she walked down the empty hallway toward the principal's office. *Have I lost my mind? What am I even doing?* She almost turned around twice, but something propelled her on. The idea of a softball team made her really excited; she didn't know why, but it was true.

As usual, Mr. Hogan's door was shut.

Emily looked at Julie, who was tapping away at her keyboard and staring at her monitor. Emily waited several seconds, and then, when Julie either didn't notice her or pretended not to, Emily took a single step toward her. It was subtle and, she thought, polite, but Julie still didn't look up. It was now obvious that the office administrator was ignoring the English teacher.

"Excuse me, Julie?"

Julie finally looked up, but she made a big show of being irritated.

"Sorry to interrupt. But do know you if Mr. Hogan's in the building?"

"If his door is shut, he's not here." She returned her gaze to the screen before she'd even finished speaking.

"OK. Do you know when he'll be back?"

"Nope," she said, eyes still straight ahead.

Trying not to be offended, or frustrated, or discouraged, Emily turned to leave the office, but as God would have it, met Mr. Hogan at the door.

"Mr. Hogan! I was just looking for you."

He didn't try to hide his annoyance. "I'm actually late for a meeting right—"

He tried to brush by her, but she followed him to his door, and didn't let him finish his sentence. "I only need thirty seconds."

"Fine," he said, unlocking the door with one of what looked like a thousand keys.

She followed him into his office and shut the door behind her. She wasn't keen to let Julie overhear what she was about to say.

"I'd like to start a softball team," she said, before he'd even sat down.

He laughed. She had expected that. "Maybe next year," he said, as if he was telling a child maybe a new bike next Christmas.

"What about this year?"

He finally looked her in the eye. "Why?" He sounded so exasperated, she almost laughed. It brought her a shameful pleasure to exasperate her principal—this might not be good.

"I have lots of reasons. Basketball is the only real option for girls here, and that's such an intense sport. Wouldn't it be great to offer a more laid back sport? It would get the kids exercising, allow more of them to be part of a team …" She saw that she was losing him, so finished with, "And because there are girls who want it."

"There are girls who want it? You mean you've already told the girls? Before you'd even mentioned it to me?"

Uh-oh. She'd gotten herself into trouble. Again. Didn't seem to matter that she never *meant* to get into trouble.

"That's not exactly how it happened," she tried.

"You know what? I don't care how it happened. The answer's still no."

"Why?" she said, even though she knew she had no grounds to ask the question, and he had no obligation to answer it.

"Why? Where do I start? The season starts in a few days—"

"A few days? It's only March 8!"

He ignored her protest. "We don't even have an athletic director"—he threw her a glance that suggested this was her fault—"and we don't have uniforms, or a field, or a schedule, or a coach—"

"I'll coach."

He raised an eyebrow. "I'm sure you would, but we don't have a budget to pay you."

"I'll coach for free. And we'll fundraise for uniforms—"

He guffawed. "You going to be the athletic director too?"

"Sure!"

His grimace suggested he was in actual physical pain.

She sat down, and leaned slightly toward his desk. "I'm sure we can just piggyback onto the baseball schedule? And so what if don't get a full schedule this year? What if we only have away games? Come on, Mr. Hogan. Let's get these girls out into the sunshine. Let's let them have some fun."

His grimace faded. She wasn't sure she'd ever seen that happen before. He almost looked persuaded. He leaned back in his chair and tipped his head from side to side as if trying to stretch out the kinks. "Fine," he finally said.

"Fine?" She failed to hide her surprise.

"I'll have to check with the superintendent and the school board. Don't tell any of the girls yet—well, don't tell them any more than you already *have*. Just keep it quiet till I get back to you."

She didn't like the sound of that. "But I'll need to start on a schedule soon. And on fundraising. When will you get back to me?"

"When I do, Miss Morse. Now your prep period is supposed to be for prepping. You may go."

She stood and smiled, sincerely. "Thanks, Mr. Hogan. Really. This is going to be a good thing. I can feel it."

Chapter 6

On Thursday, again, James took Emily to The Big Dipper for a pre-windmill meeting dinner. She waited until they'd ordered before dropping her bomb: "So I'm trying to start a softball team."

At first, he didn't react at all. Then after several seconds, he simply said, "What?"

"A softball team. I'm going to be the coach. I've got girls who want to play, and I think it will be extraordinarily fun. I'm still waiting on Mr. Hogan's OK, but I think I'm going to proceed with or without it."

James put his forearms on the table and leaned forward. "OK."

"OK? That's it?"

"Em, do you *know* anything about softball? You told me you've never played a sport in your life."

She flashed him a wide smile. "Oh, James, you can't even imagine how much I know about softball."

There was a spark in one of his eyes. Finally, he was intrigued. "Oh yeah? How's that?"

"I *grew up* on softball fields. You wouldn't believe how much time I spent at practices, games, tournaments—"

"Why?"

"Why? Well, because my dad was obsessed with softball. He played it every spring, every summer, every fall, every year of my childhood. In fact, he still plays. I just don't go anymore. He played on the church softball team, but that wasn't enough. He played on other church softball teams whenever he could, and he played in a modified fast pitch men's league that—"

"You're losing me."

"You're right. I guess you don't need his whole resumé. My point is that I didn't just hang around blooper slow pitch. I was part of an actual competitive league where the men were actually good and took it incredibly seriously."

"You were part of it?" He looked skeptical.

"Absolutely I was part of it. So in the early years, I was in a stroller. But then, I would crawl around in the dirt. Then I graduated to actually building things out of dirt and drawing in the dirt—"

"What's with all the dirt? I know you. Why didn't you just bring a book?"

"My dad wouldn't let me. He said I had to pay attention, because if my nose was buried in a book, I would get hit by a ball."

James looked skeptical again.

"I know. I think he really just wanted me to watch him play. Which I did. While I played in the dirt with my seventeen cousins."

James laughed. "What?"

"Yeah, all my dad's brothers played too. Anyway, when I was twelve, I started keeping the book, which I did faithfully until I went off to college. I'm telling you, James, I *know* softball. It's like I have all this useless knowledge bottled up in my head, that I thought would never serve a purpose, but now it will!" The pitch of her voice went up at the end, betraying her childlike excitement.

"I think girls' high school softball probably has different rules than old men's softball."

"Oh, bosh! I'll read the rulebook. Look, you don't have to be excited. I just wanted you to know." She realized then that she really didn't care if he approved or not. This thought was freeing.

"It's not that I'm not excited. I'll support you as much as I can. I'm just a little surprised."

The server returned and slid a basket of warm bread onto the table. "I'm surprised too," Emily admitted, "but it will be a good thing."

Despite getting to the windmill meeting fifteen minutes early, they almost couldn't get through the door. *And I thought the first meeting was packed.*

James took her hand and gently forced his way through the crowd, trailing her along behind him. She was so happy to hold his hand, she didn't even mind the claustrophobic feel of the people pressing in on her from all sides. She smiled and nodded to DeAnna's mother, who was sitting next to Bojack, who had an unlit cigarette hanging out of the side of his mouth. Beside him sat Sara, Duke, and Jane, her dreadlocks loose tonight and hanging all the way down to her hips.

The same cameraman was crammed into the same corner behind his tripod.

James led her to the closest wall and then wedged his shoulders into the crowd so he could lean against the wall. Then he wrapped one arm around her waist, pulling her into him so she could lean on him. Though it was at least a hundred degrees in the church, she'd never been so comfortable.

Her eyes scanned the room. She couldn't believe how many faces she'd never seen before. Yet she also felt a small pride at how many faces she did recognize. She did a quick headcount and found that most of her students were present. Thomas was in the front row, looking miserable. Chloe sat beside him.

President Darren called the meeting to order. "Thanks for coming, everyone. I know space is tight in here, but we'll get you out of here in a jiffy. I think we've all had a chance to share our opinions, and now it's time to vote—"

"We haven't all had a chance to share!" Jane said, standing up.

Darren looked exasperated. "You, Jane, have certainly had a chance—"

"I talked to a doctor from Buffalo," she said, completely ignoring Darren. She held several sheets of paper with one hand, and she struggled to unfold a pair of reading glasses with the other. Unbelievably, the crowd waited quietly for her to get her spectacles on. Then she continued, "He's an infrasound specialist, and he has given me lots of statistics to share. He has begged us—you hear me, *begged* us—to not do this to our island. He *promises* there will be serious negative side effects." She looked at the paper, cleared her throat, and began to read, "Studies show that infrasound causes fear and anxiety, the source of which the victim cannot identify, because he or she is unaware they are even hearing the sound. This anxiety can lead to mental breakdowns and violent antisocial behavior—"

"Enough!" Thomas's father stood up. "Jane, with all due respect, we're not going to ask the entire island to sit in this room while you read to us. Your unnamed expert doctor with his unnamed studies, which I assure you all, do not exist, are not going to be helpful to us here—"

"Let her talk!" Bojack called out, his lips impressively holding the unlit cigarette in place as he did so.

Jane looked down at the paper and continued, "Certain government agencies are already strategically using infrasound to cause disorientation, unease, and confusion in certain areas and certain circumstances—"

"Jane!" Travis Payne, now red-faced, said again. "Enough! Sit down—"

Vice President Bobby Snyder stood up and put a calming hand on Travis's shoulder. "Ms. Crockett, why don't you make copies of your information and distribute it to those who are interested—"

"And I'm supposed to do that before we vote tonight? Be reasonable! I have proof here that infra—"

"You don't have proof of anything, Ms. Crockett," Bobby continued. "And we would ask you to have a seat or to leave—"

"Leave?" Jane cried out. "You're going to force me to leave a town meeting?" She looked around, appalled. "Do you all hear this? Whether I'm right or wrong, don't we live in a town where we all have a chance to have a voice? Isn't this a democracy—"

"This is certainly a democracy!" Bobby raised his voice. "And that's why you get a chance to vote. What you can't do is force these people to listen to you read from a dubious source you haven't even named. We all have things to do!"

"His name is Doctor Cats, and he is an expert in ..."

Several people snickered at the good doctor's name, Emily among them. "Is the guy a veterinarian?" someone quipped from the back.

This, more than any other obstacle to her cause, seemed to frustrate Jane. "It's spelled K-A-T-Z, you imbeciles!"

"Jane, sit down right now or we will have the sheriff remove you from the room." Emily looked at Sheriff Jason Pease, who was sitting in the third pew. The sheriff wasn't really a sheriff at all; he was a deputy under the county sheriff's department, but he was the only cop on the island, he was an elected official, and he liked to be called Sheriff. So, islanders called him Sheriff. The mention of his name had startled him, and he looked reluctant to get involved, but he nodded to Bobby.

"Fine, throw me out!" Jane screeched and spread her arms out as if asking to be crucified.

"We don't want to throw you out," Bobby said, but it was getting hard to hear him as the murmuring of the crowd grew into a rumbling. "Everyone, please quiet down, we want to take this vote tonight ..." Bobby tried, but he had lost whatever modicum of control he had over the meeting.

Several people were hollering to let Jane read. A few were encouraging the sheriff to remove her. And ridiculously, Jane had begun to read from her papers again, even though no one could hear a word she said.

Emily looked at the sheriff, expecting him to do something, but he just sat there looking squeamish.

"Enough!" The female voice from the front didn't quite drown out the chaos, but still, everyone ceased their noise and looked front. Mabel Pride had stood up and was now red-faced, leaning forward on the table. "That is enough!" she said, only lowering her voice a smidge. "This is not how Piercehaven behaves. Now, this vote is going to happen tonight. It's going to happen right now. All any of you get to do is vote. That's it! You've all known this was coming. If you've had your head in the sand, then that's your fault. You've had your chance to persuade your neighbors, and that chance has passed. We are going to vote! We are going to vote right now! So sit down!"

The people who were standing, including Jane, sat down, and only a few looked reluctant. Most looked perfectly willing to submit to this woman who cheerfully took their money every month. Mabel looked down at President Darren as if waiting for him to take over. He just nodded at her to proceed. She returned her unflinching gaze to the crowd. "Please keep your hands in the air so that we can count. All in favor of Piercehaven Power installing two wind turbines on Chicken Hill, please raise one hand!"

Emily couldn't believe this was how they were going to do it. She had thought there would at least be a written vote. But apparently, everyone was going to know how everyone else voted. Thomas, despite not yet being eighteen, raised his hand. No one objected. A lot of people raised their hand. It certainly *appeared* to be a majority. President Darren, Vice-President Bobby, and Treasurer Travis all appeared to be counting hands. The room was eerily silent as they did so, as if people feared any noise would interfere with the co-op's math.

Each of the hand-counters wrote something down and then nodded at Mabel to continue.

"Thank you. You may put your hands down. Now, all opposed to the co-op putting wind turbines on Chicken Hill, please raise one hand."

Lots of hands went up, including James's. Emily hadn't noticed that he *didn't* raise his hand in favor until he *did* raise his hand in opposition. She looked at him, her eyes wide.

He looked back at her, his eyes even wider. "Aren't you going to vote?" he whispered.

It hadn't really occurred to her to vote. And it was too late now, as she would've voted yes. Clean power? Lower light bill? Wasn't it a no-brainer? She didn't really believe all the health stuff Jane had been spouting. If windmills were that dangerous, they wouldn't be popping up all over the country, right? She shook her head at James.

He frowned and looked away.

She scanned the room, and though there were a lot of hands in the air, it certainly appeared windmills were in store. And she wasn't the only one to surmise this.

"Well, prepare to start seeing ghosts," Jane said.

Chapter 7

By Monday, Emily's patience tank was dry. She went into school early and parked herself outside Mr. Hogan's closed door.

"He's not in yet," Julie said.

"I know," Emily said, trying to sound bright and cheery. "I'm just waiting."

"You could be waiting a while. I'm not sure when he'll be in."

"That's OK." She leaned against the wall.

But Julie wouldn't let it go. "Well, you'll have to go to your first period class eventually."

"Nope," Emily said. "I'm going to have class right here." Emily's tone didn't convey whether she was kidding. Emily wasn't sure whether she was kidding.

Just then, his timing so perfect it seemed orchestrated, the math teacher breezed into the office and said to Emily, "Hogan still avoiding you?"

Emily chuckled wryly. "Yep. But we've got exactly one week till pitchers and catchers start, so he can no longer avoid me. I'm going to stay right here until he gets back to me."

"Now that's the kind of commitment we want in a softball coach!" Dominic said dramatically, as he scooped a handful of junk mail out of his box.

It seemed that Julie was attempting discretion as she picked up the phone and punched some numbers. And she spoke more quietly than usual into the receiver. "Good morning. Miss Morse is here to see you. Please come in. It's urgent."

Emily attempted to kill the triumphant smile that was trying to take over her face. So Julie *could* reach the principal when she needed to. What an interesting development.

He arrived only ten minutes later, carrying a large travel mug that had steam curling off the top.

"Good morning!" Emily chirped. She realized, too late, that her cheerfulness had certainly exceeded tolerable levels. She couldn't help it, though. She felt supercharged with energy and wondered, not for the first time, if some sort of island-bound cabin fever was manifesting itself in a passion for a softball team.

"Come right in," Mr. Hogan said, before he'd even unlocked the door. She took this as a good sign.

It was.

"The school board is on board. They think it's a great idea, and the superintendent didn't object, though he might when the day comes that you no longer wish to coach for free." He sat down and relaxed into his chair as if exhausted. "We have old uniforms in the athletic locker, but I mean they are *old*—"

"We used to have a softball team?"

"Not since I've been here, and I've been here for a long time, but if the uniforms still hold together, you can use them. There might even be a bat or two, but I don't know. You'll need catcher's equipment, balls, and other stuff I'm not thinking of right now, and of course, you'll need a field. I doubt you can get all this together in time, but you're free to try."

I could've had a better shot with a longer head start, she thought. "Thanks, Mr. Hogan. I've got plenty of time."

She jumped up and bounced out of his room and started down the hall. Then she turned around and went back into the office. She was both offended and amused by the grimace her reentrance put on Julie's face. She grabbed a piece of paper out of the recycling bin and then, without asking, took a pen from Julie's desk. She wrote:

Attention ladies: Piercehaven will have a softball team this year! All girls seventh grade and up are invited to play! Please see Miss Morse to sign up.

She handed the slip of paper to Julie. "Please include this in this morning's announcements."

Julie read the message and then looked up. "Sports sign-ups are always done in the office."

"Not this time," Emily said and turned on her heel.

Chapter 8

It was difficult to get any teaching done. First period freshmen English resembled a zoo just before feeding time.

"Where will we play games?" Victoria asked. "There's no field!"

"Yes, there is, on Cobblestone Street," Caleb said. (This was an odd name for a street with no cobblestones.)

"That's not a field!" Victoria said.

"Yes, it is. There's still a backstop!" Caleb said.

"Yeah, but if you lean on it, it will fall over!" Victoria said.

Emily hadn't been aware of this field, of any field. "Who owns this field?" she asked, but no one answered her.

"What will we wear for uniforms?" Sydney asked.

"Your basketball uniforms," Tyler said, and everyone laughed. "A better question is, who on earth is going to pitch? Have you seen how those girls pitch?" Then he whipped his arm around in a hilarious attempt to demonstrate, making himself look like an uncoordinated scarecrow, and earning even more laughter from his peers.

"Caleb, do you know who owns the field?" Emily asked.

"I think the town, or the school, I mean, I think it used to be the school's field?" Caleb said, but he was looking over her shoulder at Tyler, who was now standing and pitching balled up pieces of paper across the room.

"Tyler!" Emily said, her voice completely void of anger. "Go pick those up. And stop. First, you're not allowed to try out for the softball team—"

"Sexist!" Tyler declared.

"—and second, you are going to hurt yourself."

The second period juniors weren't much calmer. And they had the same questions, for which Emily still had no answers, plus a few new ones:

"Will we go with the baseball team?" Hailey asked.

"That's my plan, but we don't actually have a schedule yet," Emily said.

"We're going to miss a lot of school," Hailey said.

"Only you would worry about that," Thomas said. Then he looked at Emily. "Can I be the manager?" This brought raucous laughter from the other boys in the room, but it appeared Thomas was serious.

"Sure," Emily said.

"Lucy asked me to sign her up," Hannah said. "Is that OK?"

"Sure," Emily said again, happy to hear a non-basketball girl's name. This made her think of DeAnna, who was sitting silently, staring down at her school-issued laptop. "How about you, DeAnna?"

She looked up at Emily, but just barely. "I don't think so."

Emily took a step closer to her and lowered her voice. "I would really like it if you would play, DeAnna. Would you reconsider?"

She shrugged. Then she asked, almost inaudibly, "Does it cost anything?"

Emily took still another step closer. "Not a penny. And I really, sincerely would enjoy having you on the team. I think it would be fun."

DeAnna looked up at her. "Why?"

"Why would it be fun?"

"No. Why do you want me to play?"

Emily sort of knew the answer to that, but it wasn't one she could share with her. She couldn't say, "I think you have a miserable life and this will give me a chance to show you some love." Nor could she say, "I'm trying to prove to my principal and my sort-of fiancé that there are girls on this island who need a softball team." So she said, "I would just enjoy getting to know you better."

The corners of DeAnna's lips moved. The expression came and went so quickly, Emily was able to talk herself out of even having seen it, but it was there. A rare DeAnna Anderson smile. "Maybe," she said.

"Tell you what. I'll sign you up. You can try it and if you don't like it, you can change your mind at any time. OK?"

"I'll have to ask my mom."

"Perfect. You do that."

It was MacKenzie in sixth period who noticed a significant pattern on the sign-up sheet:

Name	Grade	Interested in pitching or catching?
Chloe Gagnon	10	no
MacKenzie Ginn	10	no
Hailey Leadbetter	11	no
Jasmine Lane	12	no
Sydney Hopkins	9	no
Victoria Smith	9	no
Lucy Donovan	10	no
Hannah Philbrook	11	no
Ava Warren	12	no
Natalie Greem	12	no
Kylie Greem	7	no
Allie Cousens	12	no
Lily Coombs	7	no
Zoe Lane	8	no
DeAnna Anderson	11	no
Sara Crockett	10	no

"Um, Miss M? You have no pitcher," MacKenzie said worriedly.

"Yeah, I've noticed that. Don't worry. We'll figure it out."

"We will?" MacKenzie looked doubtful. "Isn't pitching kind of hard?"

"Not really. It's only difficult to be good at it."

The class laughed at this, though Emily hadn't been trying for humor, but MacKenzie didn't even start to smile. "You're not going to make me do it, are you?"

Emily walked over to her desk and softly said, "No. You can't pitch. You're the catcher. Now please take out your short story."

"What? Why?"

"Why do I want you to take out your short story? Because this is English class."

MacKenzie gave her a scowl that was now so familiar to Emily it had become endearing. "You know what I mean."

"In softball, the catcher runs the field. The catcher has to be tough, smart, and able to lead. I need to make sure you can catch the ball, but I'm pretty sure you can. Then you'll be my catcher."

MacKenzie looked at her for a moment longer and then looked down at the sign-up sheet. She erased her "no" and replaced it with an "I'll try."

"Those are the miracle words, my dear MacKenzie."

Chapter 9

As soon as that final bell sounded, Emily was on the phone with athletic directors all over the state. Most were happy to hear her news, a few sounded skeptical, and one was downright patronizing. Tim Whittemore from Richmond: "Are you *sure* you want to play us the first year? You *know* we were state champs last year, right?" Emily had no idea. She hadn't cared about such things a year ago. She barely cared now.

"You can say no," she reminded him.

He backpedaled a little. "I'm not saying no. I just want you to know what you'll be up against. Frankly, it could be a slaughter."

Emily rubbed her temple, where a small throb had taken root. "I'm sure your coach will respond accordingly. Maybe it will give him or her a chance to play his subs."

"Coach," he said, his condescension almost palpable through the phone line, "our *subs* will slaughter you."

"Like I said, you can say no. But if not, we'll see you on the twenty-first."

"Well, you won't see *me*." He chortled. He was far too important to be coaching a softball team. "But you'll be seeing our team. Good luck."

Emily hung up the phone and took a deep breath. She now had two home games scheduled. Even though she had no field. How hard could a field be?

"How hard can a field be?" James repeated, clearly astonished. "You realize you're sitting on a giant rock, right?"

She was also sitting on a barstool. The Big Dipper was busy and there had been no tables available. So she was bellied up to the bar, showing the man of her dreams her new softball schedule.

"Well, the kids told me there used to be a field on Cobblestone Street. So maybe someone hauled in some sod a few decades ago?"

James gave her a look that said he didn't appreciate her tone. "Have you seen that supposed field?"

"No, but I hear there's a backstop."

"Yep, a dilapidated death trap that wouldn't stop a tennis ball. And the field has turned into a group latrine for all the neighborhood dogs."

"Ew!" she said, and meant it. "Let's go take a look at it after we eat."

He looked at her again, but this time she thought she saw a twinkle of admiration in his eyes. "You are like a dog after a bone."

"Just what every woman wants to hear from her ..." She stopped herself. She didn't know what to call him. Boyfriend? Fiancé? Platonic dining partner?

He didn't come to her rescue. He just picked up his soda and drank through his straw, blankly gazing at the television behind the bar.

After an eternity, their burgers came, and they ate in a silence that became less uncomfortable as it went on. By the time he was wiping ketchup from his lips and asking for the check, things were back to normal.

"So can we?" she asked.

"What?" He stood and grabbed his coat. Then he remembered. "Oh yeah, the field. Sure, let's go take a look." He paid the tab and they headed outside into the cold.

"Hard to believe we'll be playing anything outside soon. It's freezing out here." She tightened her scarf.

"It will probably be cold for your first few games too. Though you're away your first weekend, right? It will be warmer in Buckfield. Less wind."

She grinned. "So you *did* pay attention to my shiny new schedule."

"Ah, yes," he said, opening the pickup door for her. "I can't even tell you how enthusiastic I am about your softball season."

She thought he was being ironic, but his deadpan tone gave nothing away.

Though she was determined not to let the sight of the old softball field—no matter its condition—discourage her, she couldn't help it. It wasn't a softball field at all.

"Why have they even bothered to keep cutting the grass?" she muttered.

"For the dogs, I think," he said, taking her hand as she slid out of the truck.

This small touch cheered her up. But then she looked at the field again. "Did they used to have a grass infield?"

He squinted. "I think … and I'm really stretching here, as I don't remember spending any time here, that the base paths were dirt, but the rest was grass. But I could be getting it confused with the baseball field. Sorry." He walked over to the backstop and pushed on it.

It wobbled, but didn't come crashing down. "I can build you a backstop."

This shocked her. "You can?"

He chuckled. "Sure. I don't want to. But I love you. And this will be good for the girls."

"Can you skin an infield too?"

He scowled. "I don't know what that means."

"It means, can you peel the sod off the infield, so I can have a dirt infield?"

He didn't look excited about this. "What kind of equipment do they use for that?"

"I have no idea."

He nodded but it looked reluctant. "I don't know any of the measurements."

"That's OK," she said quickly, "I've already emailed the MPA and asked them to send me a rulebook. I'm sure the requirements are in there."

He groaned. "I'm sure they are." He looked at the giant boulder sticking out of deep center field. "Don't most fields have a fence?"

"Yes, but let's do one thing at a time."

Chapter 10

She got to school early on Tuesday to explore the athletic locker. Which was, of course, locked. To unlock the locker meant contact with Larry—the world's crankiest custodian. Just the thought of having to converse with him made her sick with dread. Still, in the name of that small neon yellow ball, she went in search of him.

It should have been easy to find the only custodian in the smallest school in the state—but it wasn't. She finally deduced that he wasn't there yet and resigned herself to sit and wait by the athletic locker like some sort of aging gym rat. She'd almost nodded off in the warm gym when she saw the lights flicker on in the main office.

She got up and padded across the small gym/cafeteria, crossed the empty hallway, and entered the main office. "Good morning, Julie."

Julie looked up. "Morning. You're here early." No smile within a mile.

"Yes, I'm looking for Larry. Do you know what time he gets in?"

Julie spared her a glance and then sat down and looked at her still sleeping monitor. "He's probably been here for an hour by now."

"Are you sure? I've looked everywhere—"

"Yes," she said, now glaring at Emily. "Of course I'm sure. I've worked here for twenty years. So has he. And his truck is in the parking lot."

Emily was offended and tried not to be. "I apologize. Let's start over. I need to find Larry. Can you tell me where he is?"

"Why do you need to find him?"

This was none of her business, of course, but Emily was already losing this battle, and she knew it. "I need to get into the athletic locker."

Julie opened a drawer beside her, reached in without looking, and came out with a key. "Here you go. Don't forget to bring it back. New teachers are always quitting without returning their keys. There are probably a hundred master keys floating around this fine state of ours."

Then why do we bother to lock anything? Emily thought, but she smiled and said, "Thank you. I'll bring it right back."

The locker smelled like sweaty socks and pickle juice. She fumbled for a light switch, skinning her knuckles on unidentified hard plastic artifacts until the string dangling from the ceiling brushed against her collarbone and nearly made her shriek. Her first thought was that it was a spider web, but when she gave it a yank, it lit up the small room and revealed nary a spider in sight. There wasn't room for one.

Trunks were stacked upon trunks, each trunk labeled by something illegible scrawled across yellowed athletic tape. The top trunk held basketball uniforms. Surprise. The one beneath that—basketball uniforms. The one beneath that—prom gowns. She could hardly believe that's what she was seeing, but there it was.

She moved these trunks out into the gym, which created enough room in the locker so that she could then turn around. Next she wheeled out the basketball bin, its wheels creaking in protest as if to suggest she didn't have the right.

Behind the basketballs were two large equipment bags. Unzipping them (and then tucking her nose inside her shirt) revealed the school's baseball equipment—quite a bit of it. She carried it out into the gym. Underneath the bags was a trunk of baseball uniforms and two buckets of balls. She was getting warmer.

Next she found a pitching machine buried in a pile of netting that could only be a collapsed batting cage. But when she slid the pitching machine aside, a pile of floor hockey sticks hit the cement floor with a terrific crash. She cringed, waiting for the jangle of Larry's keys, but it never came, so she resumed her excavation. Some folding metal chairs, three flat soccer balls, one rock hard football, and finally: softball bats. Two of them. Leaning on yet another trunk, this one shoved so far under some shelving that she hadn't even seen it. Could this be it? She dragged it into the light.

And there they were. Softball uniforms. A wave of warm peace flowed through her. Or maybe it was sweat. She dragged the new trunk out into the gym and then stood and wiped her brow. Only then did she begin to worry she'd never be able to get all this stuff back into the locker. Oh well, she wasn't sure there was anyone left to scold her for such a trespass. The sex-offender athletic director was long gone.

Another foray into the locker found tennis rackets, boomerangs, dodge balls, medicine balls, and oddly, a stack of pillowcases. But no softball catching equipment. No softball batting helmets. And no softballs.

As she slid the odds and ends back into place, she was almost discouraged. *I'm really going to have to fundraise. I don't want to do a bottle drive.* There was no redemption center on the island. She shuddered at the thought of her small car packed full of stinky returnables on the ferry. She thought about asking her church for help, but didn't think they would be able to. Half of them were fishermen, coming off a long winter of no fishing. She knew many of them were struggling. Leaving the softball uniforms and two bats immediately in front of the door, she turned off the light and closed up, grateful the door did in fact click shut. Then she turned to return the key to the office despot.

Chapter 11

"Did you see Crazy Jane's letter in the paper?" Thomas asked Emily.

"Never mind that," Chloe said. "Do we have a softball schedule?"

"Sort of. I've got ten games, but I also left messages with Vinalhaven and Valley. So we'll probably play them too. Basically, we're just going where the baseball team goes."

"Do you think we could have a scrimmage with someone?" Chloe asked.

"What do you mean?"

"I mean"—Chloe looked around the room as if to confirm it was just the three of them—"well, we are not exactly used to being *bad* at something, and I think maybe we're going to be kind of bad at this. So I was thinking maybe we could have a practice game against someone, before a real game that counts?"

Emily's first thought was to find a church softball team to come scrimmage them, but Thomas interrupted her train of thought.

"Camden Christian is close," he said, "and they're never good at anything. They might scrimmage us."

"Thomas, that's not a very encouraging thing to say. And also, don't call Jane crazy. I don't think she's crazy at all."

"You haven't seen her in her tinfoil hat."

"Really?" Emily had bought it.

Thomas laughed.

"So did you find uniforms?" Chloe asked.

"Sure did."

"Can I see them?"

"Sure. Meet me in the gym after school."

"Do you know who is going to pitch?"

"Nope. You interested?"

She shrugged. "I'll try it. But I don't know if any of us are going to be able to do it. I was watching pitchers on YouTube last night. It's pretty crazy."

"Well, you were watching *good* pitchers on YouTube. You weren't watching Maine Class D high school pitchers."

"I was watching Richmond."

"Oh."

The bell rang and Emily's first period freshmen began wandering into the room. Chloe stood to go. Then she turned back. "By the way, how did you get Sara Crockett to sign up for softball?"

It was Emily's turn to shrug. "I didn't do anything. She just signed up."

Thomas held out his fist for a bump. "I'm serious, Miss M, read Jane's letter. She is going to cause a lot of trouble. I'm not so sure you want her kid on your team."

Emily sighed. "Makes me worry about Duke and Sara. How does Jane's passion affect them?"

"Don't worry about Duke," Thomas said. "He's just as nuts as his mother. Acts like windmills are pure evil." He put his hands up in the air for the last few words and shook them like jazz hands, adding a trill in his voice for dramatic effect.

"Go to class, Thomas," Emily said, firmly but with affection.

Emily finally got a chance to Google Jane's opinion piece during her fifth period prep. The letter was lengthy and well-written. Jane certainly had a firmer grasp of the English language than her son. *Or*, Emily wondered, *does Duke just have me fooled*? The letter was vehement, but there was really nothing new. It was more of what Jane had already said at the town meetings: windmills pose health hazards; windmills ruin island scenery; windmills make people see ghosts ... Wait! This was something new. Windmills also caused pets to exhibit behavioral issues. Emily rolled her eyes and scanned the rest of the article. Jane ended with an enigmatic "This battle isn't over. Piercehaven is not going to let these monstrosities go up." *Is that a threat?*

Emily's eyes flicked to the comments, and they were numerous (425 and counting) and brutal. And there was no way *all* the commenters were islanders. She just couldn't see that many Piercehaveners taking the time to log on and comment. No, Jane was attracting attention from around the state, and maybe even beyond.

A few commenters claimed to be from Vinalhaven. One of them encouraged Jane to stand strong and protect her island. The other told Jane to stop whining and causing drama.

Emily winced at how many of the comments were personally directed at Jane. How could people be so cruel? *Ah the bravery internet anonymity allows*, Emily thought and forced herself to close the window.

Chloe brought friends to her afterschool meeting with Emily. Hailey, MacKenzie, and surprisingly, Sara accompanied Chloe across the gym.

Emily unlocked the athletic locker for the second time that day and then asked Chloe to run the key back to Julie. Chloe obliged.

Emily flipped open the trunk and pulled out the top uniform.

Hailey grimaced. "Miss M, it's *striped*!"

Emily looked down at the uniforms and then at Hailey. "So?"

"So? So they're ugly!"

"Oh, come on," Emily said, "they're not so bad."

MacKenzie reached into the trunk and grabbed a uniform. Then she held it out in front of her and shook it until it unfolded. "Eeewww."

"Oh, stop it. At least we have uniforms," Emily said. "I repeat. They're not bad."

"But why do they have little red stripes up and down them?" MacKenzie asked. "We're going to look like candy canes!"

Chloe returned then. "Yikes. Those are pretty bad."

Emily really didn't see the issue. They weren't that bad, and she knew they could be *much* worse.

"They're *scratchy*," MacKenzie whined.

"You guys need to stop. These are fine. I'll see what I can do about getting new ones, but that's going to take some time. For now, let's do the best we can with what we've got."

Sara, who hadn't made a peep, reached into the trunk and pulled out a red stirrup. "What the heck is this thing?" She held it up to her face and peered out through the hole made by the straps. "Is it a thong?"

The girls laughed as though this were the funniest thing they'd ever heard. Emily had to struggle to keep a straight face. She ripped the stirrup out of Sara's hands and said, "It's a stirrup and we don't have to wear them. We can just wear socks."

MacKenzie had already grabbed another stirrup from the trunk and was pretending it was a slingshot. "No, I think we should use them! They're like little polyester weapons!"

Chapter 12

Emily and Kyle had lunch duty. They leaned against the padded gym walls and stared silently out at the dining adolescents. She had just heard, and chosen to ignore, the third f-bomb of the period. "You know," she said, trying to make conversation, "the biggest argument against homeschooling is that kids won't learn social skills—but, do you see great social skills here?"

Kyle looked at her. "You going to homeschool?"

"No, but there are families in my church who do, and I can't say I blame them."

Kyle snorted. "Religious fanatics. I'd find another church, Em."

She bristled more at him calling her Em than she did at the fanatics comment. "They're not fanatics," she said. *And I'm not your friend so don't call me Em*, she thought. Then, *although, I did start this conversation so it's my own fault.*

"Whatever you say," he said without looking at her.

"I know them. They're not fanatics. And they don't homeschool because of religion. They homeschool because they are trying to protect their children.

"From what?"

"From this!" She pointed at the students she loved so much: at Duke, who was currently flipping someone off; at Tyler, who had just dropped a hamburger bun and was now intentionally grinding it into the floor with his heel; at freshman Sydney, who had her hands so far up senior Blake's leg that Emily knew she should intervene; at DeAnna, who sat ostracized at her own table, though there were only six tables in the whole cafeteria.

"You might have a point," Kyle admitted. "But I still don't think homeschooling is the answer."

"Excuse me," a voice on the other side of Kyle said. "Are you Miss Morse?"

Emily looked around Kyle and up into the face of an exceptionally attractive man. Dark brown locks fell over his tan forehead and into one of his chocolate brown eyes, almost touching his sharp, high cheekbones.

"I am," she said, grateful her voice didn't shake. She blinked, thought of James, and completely recovered. "I am," she said again. "How can I help you?"

"Do you have a moment?" he said, looking at Kyle as if he wanted him to go away.

"Sure, let's step outside," she said. They stepped out into the hallway, where Larry was lurking, so she continued walking. "Let's go into the conference room." She entered the empty room and flicked on the lights, but she didn't shut the door. She had learned a lot from James, and knew it wasn't wise to be alone in a room with a man, especially one who looked like this.

He cleared his throat and stuck out his hand. "I'm Jake Jasper. I've just moved to the island, for a while at least. I'm going to be the foreman at the wind turbine site."

"Oh!" Emily exclaimed. "Well, then, welcome to the island!"

He smiled, revealing ridiculously straight, white teeth. "Thank you. I wanted to talk to you about my daughter, Juniper. She'll be starting here tomorrow. She's a junior, and they tell me you're the softball coach."

This perked her up. "I am! Tell me she's a pitcher."

He scrunched his eyebrows together. "You need a pitcher?"

"Indeed we do."

"Well, that might help. But she also plays third."

"Help what?"

"Juniper is furious with me." He took a deep breath and a half step back. Then he put his hands on his hips and looked at the floor. "It's kind of a long story, but Juniper's mom left a while back, and so now it's just the two of us. I used to travel a lot for work, and so, we don't have the best relationship. And well"—he looked at her—"I just uprooted my teenage daughter from her hometown, all her friends, and her class A softball team, and I moved her to the middle of the ocean, where she said there wasn't even a softball team." He looked confused.

"She was right. There didn't used to be. This is our first year."

His jaw clenched. "Well, I suppose that's better than nothing."

"It is. I'm sorry that we won't be what she's used to, but we *will* have fun, and we would love to have her. Even if she's not a pitcher."

"Oh, she is. She's amazing. But she's also copping a major attitude since her mom left. I mean, she was no saint before. But since our split, her grades have slid, and she started hanging out with different kids … I think just to irritate me … another reason leaving

Mattawooptock was a good idea ... sorry, I'm babbling."

"Mattawooptock?" Emily asked. Even without paying attention, Emily knew that Mattawooptock was one of the strongest softball programs in the state.

"Yep. She wasn't the starting pitcher, but she might get the spot next year. She says she would have had it this year, but I think that's a stretch." He paused, and then hastened to add, "Not that I'm asking you to let her pitch, or start her, or anything. I just wanted to give you a heads up before she shows up tomorrow copping major attitude and acting like she's too good for your team. I wanted you to know I am completely aware of her antics, and will support the school in dealing with them. Don't hesitate to call me when you have issues, because ... I think you will."

"Well!" Emily said, unsure of what to say next. This was the most pleasant parent conference she'd ever had. When it wasn't necessary to defend herself, she wasn't sure how to respond. "Thank you for coming in. I think she'll be fine, really. We'll take good care of her, and she'll adjust. There are some great kids here, and I'll ask a few of them to help make her feel welcome."

His face lit up. "I hadn't even thought to ask that. Thanks." He nodded, there was an awkward pause, and then he stuck out his hand. "Thank you, Miss Morse. I mean it."

She shook his hand. "Emily, please. And you're welcome."

Emily didn't get a chance to talk to Thomas and Chloe together, alone, until the following morning. "I have a big favor to ask of you two."

Chloe looked thrilled.

Thomas looked suspicious. "Does this have anything to do with the stupid windmills?"

"No, why?" Emily asked, surprised.

"Because people are prank calling my house all night long. And Marget is refusing to sell our family groceries. Big whoop. Like we're not perfectly capable of going to the mainland and saving zillions of dollars *not* shopping at her stupid store."

Emily stared at him, unsure of what to say. "Well, maybe it's *indirectly* related to the windmills."

Thomas groaned.

"What is it, Miss M?" Chloe asked.

"We're getting a new girl today. And I need you two to befriend her, make her feel welcome—it's not easy being the new kid here. I speak from experience."

"Fine," Thomas said. "Is she hot?"

Chloe jammed her elbow into his ribs. Hard.

"Ow!" he cried. But his eyes were sparkling.

"I have no idea if she's attractive, but I need you to be nice to her either way." Emily looked at Chloe. "She's probably going to play softball."

Chloe's eyes lit up. "I'm on it, Miss Morse." She looked at Thomas, then back at Emily. "*We're* on it. Piece of cake. I'll even invite her to church."

Thomas groaned again.

"Great. Thanks. And don't forget to keep inviting Thomas too. Now, she's a junior, so you'll be with her all day, Thomas. Her name is Juniper."

Thomas swore. Then, "Sorry, Miss M. I just … I didn't realize she was here already. That's the windmill chick." He spoke the words with gravity, as if he were announcing an impending viral outbreak.

"So?" Emily asked.

"So?" Thomas cried, incredulous. "So you're asking the *current* punching bag of all windmill hatred to take care of the *future* punching bag of windmill hatred? You really didn't think this through, did you?"

Chloe looked at Thomas. "How do you already know about her?"

"Because her dad is renting one of our apartments. And because my parents told me about them. But I didn't think they were here yet. This is going to suck so bad."

Emily leaned forward in her chair. "Sounds like you and Juniper might need each other."

Chloe flushed red, just a little. "It'll be fine, Miss M. Don't forget, Thomas is a drama queen."

Emily thought maybe Chloe was feeling a little jealous, and hurried to redirect. "I just thought this was a good task for you two. You're the popular kids around here."

Thomas snorted. "I'm not sure any fish is popular in a mud puddle, Miss Morse."

Chapter 13

The boys went crazy. And in a very different way, so did the girls.

Juniper was gorgeous. Long, wavy, thick dark hair. Flawless skin. Curves in the right places. Everywhere she went, the boys' eyes followed. As they goggled at her, the girls glared at them. It was a corporate stare down, and no one was winning.

On Thursday morning, Juniper showed up early, with her dad, and picked up her schedule and locker combination from Julie. Then Jake Jasper vanished, leaving her to find her locker alone. Emily approached her then, impressed that Juniper was able to get the locker open on the first try. These were some really old, dented, abused, sticky lockers.

"Hi, Juniper. Welcome to our little school. My name is Miss Morse."

Juniper gave her a disgusted look, but didn't say anything.

"My classroom is the last one on the left, and you are welcome there anytime. If you need anything, just pop in."

Juniper returned her gaze to the inside of her empty locker. "I won't be here long enough to need anything." She slammed the locker door and looked at Emily. "But thanks," she said, not sounding as if she meant it.

"I'm also the softball coach. Hoping you'll play for us?"

Juniper looked her up and down. "I've heard about your softball team," she said with disdain. "No thanks. Can you tell me which room is math?"

Emily pointed.

"Thanks," she said, again sounding entirely ungrateful.

Trying not to be offended, Emily made her way to her classroom to wait for Thomas and Chloe.

She didn't have to wait long.

"Well, Miss M," Thomas began. "I was willing to help Juniper out, but I can't get close to her. Blake is all over her."

"I thought Blake was going out with Sydney?"

"Not for long, I think," Thomas said.

"I don't think the infatuation will last long," Chloe said. "Juniper is a ..." She trailed off, looking at Emily. "Well, she's not a very nice girl."

"She just got here. She doesn't want to be here. Give her some time," Emily said.

"Time?" Chloe said, indignant. "Hailey just asked her if she was going to play softball, and she flipped Hailey off."

Emily raised an eyebrow. "Well, that's not good."

Thomas was laughing.

"What?" Chloe snapped.

"Nothing, really. It's just, life is so boring around here. This is the first part of the windmill drama I'm actually going to enjoy."

"Why is her father here already, anyway?" Chloe asked.

"They're starting. They're excavating the land right now. He's supervising. More men are arriving every day."

"How is this all happening so fast?" Emily asked. "The vote just passed."

"The vote was just a formality. Because, technically, Piercehaven Power is a cooperative. But the wheels have been in motion for a while."

"I see," Emily said thoughtfully. "So then there must already be a plan for where all these windmill workers are going to stay?"

"Didn't you hear?" Thomas asked, his tongue in his cheek. "You're hosting."

"Don't be a wise guy," Emily said with affection.

"No, they're all staying in our apartments. Most of them are doubling and tripling up."

"I didn't realize you had so many apartments, Thomas."

"Well, we used to only have two buildings, and those were pretty much full, so my dad has bought two more in the last two years, getting ready for this."

"He knew this was coming two years ago?"

"It was only a matter of time before the land became his. Grandma owned the highest land on the island. He knew that once he owned it, he'd try to get wind power up. I'm pretty sure he's been planning this since Vinalhaven put theirs up."

"Why? Why is he so devoted to wind power?"

Thomas held up his right hand and rubbed his thumb against his fingertips. "It's all about the moola, Miss M. My dad is a businessman."

"Is he really going to make *that* much money off this?" Emily didn't understand.

"He's going to make more than my grandmother did just letting the land sit there."

"I'm surprised she never sold it, if she didn't want it for anything," Emily said.

"It's been in the family forever. Islanders don't sell their land. If they do, they're hated for it."

"Why?" Emily was appalled at the thought.

"Because people from away buy the land. And then they come here." He looked at her as if she were dense. "And that's not good."

"Why?" Emily asked, even though she was starting to get the picture.

"Because we *don't like* people from away. Because we're *Piercehaven*," Thomas said.

"You like me?" Emily said.

"You don't count," Thomas and Chloe said in unison.

Juniper was in Emily's second period class, and she was at least as unpleasant as she had been for their introduction. There was lots of sighing and eye rolling—and no eye contact. Emily had to tell her to put her phone away three times. When Emily said, "Everyone, this is Juniper. Welcome to Piercehaven, Juniper," Juniper replied, "No thanks."

When Emily handed out a Lucille Clifton poem, Juniper refused to look at it. She continued her refusal as the class discussed it, and when Emily asked, "Why do you think the poet chose to use boats as a metaphor, Juniper?" Juniper replied, "Don't care." At the bell, she got up so fast that she caused a wind, which blew the poem to the floor, where she left it. *She's obviously not planning on doing the homework*, Emily thought, beyond annoyed.

Emily cheered up when she found a softball rulebook in her mailbox. *The MPA is certainly on their toes*. She carried the small book into the gym for lunch duty but then forgot about it as she watched the male population of Piercehaven High watch Juniper go through the line. They stared at her as she stared at her phone, but then she put it into her back pocket as she held her tray out for a floppy slice of pizza. Then, remarkably, she made her way to the emptiest table in the place and wordlessly sat down kitty corner from DeAnna, who looked up at her and then jerked her head back down toward her tray.

Juniper didn't look at her.

Emily walked over to the table and sat down opposite Juniper. "Hi, Juniper."

Juniper didn't acknowledge her.

"I understand that you don't want to be—"

"You don't understand anything," Juniper snapped.

"I understand," Emily repeated, "that you don't want to be here. But you *are* here. So maybe you should make the best of it. You can choose not to be miserable, you know."

Juniper took out her phone and looked at it. "Who says I'm miserable?"

"Well, there are a bunch of cool kids, kids worth getting to know, in this school, and you're spending all your time staring at a phone—"

"Just stop. I don't want to bond with you. Leave me alone."

Emily paused, trying to decide what to say next. She was about to silently pray for assistance when words came out. "Juniper, this is my first year here, and I promise you, this is not an easy place to be new. You're going to need someone on your side. When that time comes, I'll be here." Then, before Juniper could respond, Emily stood and walked away.

Kyle said something to her as she passed, and though she thought he was asking about what had just transpired, she didn't hear him, nor did she slow or stop her stride. She had to get to the staff restroom. Because she was crying.

After she got a grip, she ditched lunch duty and went to her room to Google a phone number. Then she walked the entire length of the school again, back by the cafeteria, and into the teachers' room, where several teachers were eating. This surprised her. She hadn't realized teachers actually ate together in the teachers' room. She had thought it was just a place for the coffee pot and the phone. (She always ate lunch alone in her room during her prep, while she graded papers.) Emily greeted her colleagues with a nod, hoped her eyes weren't red enough to be telltale, and dialed the number.

"Mattawooptock High School, how may I help you?"

"Hi, yes, I'm trying to get in touch with your softball coach."

"Which one?" the voice on the other line said, her tone flavored with snark.

"Sorry, the varsity coach."

"Who is this?"

"This is the Piercehaven softball coach."

"Oh!" she said, as if she had solved all the mysteries of the universe. "Well, he's not here right now. He doesn't work at the school. But I can take a message and ask him to call you back?"

"Sure." Emily provided her name and the school's number. Then she added her home phone number, just in case. She hung up, feeling impatient. She wasn't sure how this man would be able to help, but she didn't see how he couldn't.

Chapter 14

Emily curled up on her couch with a cup of tea and the softball rulebook. Nick Carraway, her male tabby, curled up in her lap. Daisy Buchanan, her female tabby, curled up on the back of the couch and looked out the window.

The rules were remarkably similar to men's softball, though she couldn't remember any man sprinting to first after striking out. Just the thought made her giggle.

She was dismayed to see that high school bats had to have an ASA Certified stamp on them. She didn't even have to look at the relics she'd found to know they had no such stamp. She was going to have to start fundraising. Pitchers and catchers were to start Monday; the rest of the team, the following Monday.

She decided to have a team meeting the next day. As she was thinking about how to raise funds in a community with no funds, her landline rang. She jumped up, thinking it was

James. He was the only one who called her—him and the debt collectors looking for the previous tenant. No matter how many times she told them that Alec Pratt didn't live there anymore, they didn't believe her.

"Hello?"

"Hi, this is Danny Kirk."

It took her brain a few seconds to recognize the name, but when she did, she was thrilled to hear the voice. "Hi, Coach. Thanks so much for returning my call. I wanted to talk to you about Juniper Jasper. She has moved—"

"I know. I wasn't surprised to get your message. You're going to have your hands full."

"Well, I'm thrilled to have her. This is a brand-new program, and we're happy to have someone who's played the game, but she isn't exactly thrilled to be here. In fact, she says she doesn't even want to play."

"If she doesn't play, I'll eat my hat. That girl loves softball. But you're going to have to set some firm boundaries or she'll try to run the show. She's a confident young lady and she can be mouthy. I've had to bench her before. But once I let her know she wouldn't disrespect me or her teammates, she toed the line."

Emily sighed, unsure of how to respond.

Coach Kirk didn't let her. "She's a good kid, really, she is. She's just … volatile, and if you have a new program, she's probably not going to be very patient. But I think if you don't let her push you around, she'll respect you for it."

"Easier said than done."

"Absolutely. If you have any specific situations, give me a shout, anytime."

"Thanks. I will do that. What's the best time to call you? I don't want to interrupt you at work."

"I work in the woods. So you can usually get me on my cell. Might not hear you over the saw, but I'll get right back to you."

Emily wrote down his cell number and thanked him profusely before hanging up. Then she returned to her couch, lay down, and proceeded to memorize the rulebook.

The next morning, Emily asked Julie to announce that there would be a softball team meeting during lunch.

"No one does that," Julie said.

"OK, well, I'm doing it. Please ask all the softball players to sit at my table."

As Emily walked away, she could still hear Julie muttering, "If no one does that, there's a reason no one does that …"

Thomas showed up in Emily's doorway alone.

"Where's Chloe?"

"I think she's mad at me."

"Why?"

"I gave Juniper a ride to school today. Chloe was pretty cranky about it. Then when we got here, she disappeared. Not sure where she is."

"You still gave Chloe a ride too, right?"

"Yep." Thomas collapsed into a chair on the other side of her desk. "But I didn't tell Chloe first, so when she got to the car, and Juniper was in the front, Chloe was all mad." He shook his head. "Girls."

"How's Juniper?"

"How should I know?"

"I'm not accusing you of anything, Thomas. But you just saw her. How did she seem? Better? Happy? Miserable?"

"I would say she's holding steady at miserable."

"Ah, perfect."

Thomas hung out till the bell rang, but Chloe never appeared. In fact, Emily didn't lay eyes on her until the lunch line. On her way to DeAnna's table, Emily passed Chloe and whispered, "You OK?"

Chloe shrugged. "Why wouldn't I be?"

"I just didn't see you this morning. Thomas mentioned you might be upset about something."

"Yeah, well, Thomas is an idiot," she said, and took several steps forward in line.

Emily sat down at DeAnna's table only seconds before she got there.

"What are you doing?" DeAnna asked.

"Didn't you hear the announcement? We're having a softball meeting."

"At this table?"

"That's right. You're part of the team, right?"

DeAnna looked around like a scared rabbit. "I don't know—"

"Just sit, DeAnna. Relax. I've got your back."

MacKenzie joined them next. Then Hannah. Then Chloe. Then Thomas.

"Thomas?" Emily said.

"I'm the manager, aren't I?" Thomas asked. Then he nudged Chloe with his hip. "Slide over, Chloe." She slid over without looking at him, but Emily sensed she was pleased with the interaction.

Then they came in a swarm—all but Juniper. Emily got up to make room for them. She glanced at Juniper sitting by herself at a different table, her back to the team. She thought maybe Juniper wanted her to beg, so she decided not to. She had wanted a softball team back before they had a ringer from Mattawooptock; she still wanted them now, even if they were going to be terrible.

"OK, ladies. Just wanted to discuss a few things with you," she said, loudly enough for Juniper to hear. "First, we have a full schedule. Wherever the baseball team goes, we follow. Pitchers and catchers start Monday. We're sharing the gym with the boys, so we won't start practice until four. Please try to have a glove by then, because I want you all to show up for pitchers and catchers. We have no idea who will be playing where, so let's all try out each of those positions. OK?" She didn't wait for them to agree. "Now, we have a schedule, we have some uniforms, we sort of have a field, but—"

"What field?" Hannah asked, but Emily ignored her.

"—we don't yet have any equipment. We need some bats, some balls, some bases, and some catcher's gear, and we have no budget. So that means fundraisers!" She raised her voice to a ridiculous pitch to fake excitement. *If you can't genuinely be excited about something, might as well fake it and hope for a laugh.*

No one laughed.

"You won't be able to raise any money, Miss M," Thomas said.

"Well, that may be. But we have to try. So, who has fundraising ideas?"

The carwash was vetoed because no one on Piercehaven washed their vehicles. The bake sale was vetoed because none of the girls knew how to bake anything and didn't think their mothers did either. The bottle drive was vetoed (for this Emily was relieved) because everyone already gave their returnables to the nursing home. A spaghetti supper was a possibility, and Hailey promised to ask Marget if she would donate noodles and sauce.

Promptly after the last bell of the day, Thomas appeared in Emily's doorway.

"Hey, what's up?" she asked, sincerely delighted to see him.

"You don't have to fundraise."

"I know it'll be difficult, but we've got to—"

"No, I mean you really don't. I called my dad and he said to just tell him how much you need."

It took a while for this to sink in. "Seriously?"

Thomas nodded. "Of course, he wants full credit, you know, mention him at the banquet, and in your championship speech ..."

She laughed.

"But yeah, he said to just give him a number and he'll write a check. He's not a bad guy, really."

Chapter 15

James picked Emily up at six o'clock on Saturday night for a big night out on the town. They were going to The Big Dipper. But first, James took a detour.

"Where are we going?"

"I thought a stroll along the cobblestones might be romantic."

Emily laughed. "Were there *ever* cobblestones on Cobblestone Street?"

"There must have been. But I don't know. I'm not *that* old."

Emily laughed again and looked out the window. She couldn't imagine why he was taking her back to the field. She'd only given him the rulebook's measurements the afternoon before. Unless he'd spent all day at the field.

That's just what he'd done. Although he hadn't done it alone. He pulled up next to the field, behind a truck she recognized as belonging to Abe Cafferty. Abe and his son,

Noah, were both standing on the first base line, smiling.

She slid out of the truck in a daze. "James, how did you do this so fast?"

"We worked all day. The snow's gone, so unless we get more, which we might," he said in a portending tone, "you'll be able to practice outside soon. So, you needed a field. And a backstop," he added, his eyes sparkling as he glanced at the new backstop.

She walked over to it and then couldn't help herself—she leaned on it. It didn't budge. Solid as a rock.

There were no dugouts, but each team now had a bench, and those too looked incredibly solid.

"James," she said, and then remembered he wasn't the only one there. "Guys! I don't know what to say."

"We didn't really do it for you, honey," James said. "We did it for the girls, for the island. And we're still going to try to get a fence up." He glanced at the boulder in center field. "I don't think anybody is going to hit it that far, but just in case ..."

"Hey, don't count MacKenzie out," Noah said, obviously proud that his girlfriend would be wearing the Panther pinstripes.

James had already finished his supper and Emily was almost done when they saw the sheriff's car go by the restaurant with lights flashing and siren blaring. They looked at each other.

"Well, that's not something you see every day," Emily said.

"I don't think I've *ever* seen that," James said. Then he looked at her mischievously. "Want to follow him?"

"Seriously?"

He didn't wait for an answer. He got up, put a twenty on the table, and grabbed his coat. "Come on."

She stood up. "Hang on," she said, "it's not like we're going to lose him. This is an island." She grabbed her coat and several final fries, and followed him to the door.

At first, it appeared they *had* lost him, but it soon became evident they were not the only ones who had this idea. There were too many vehicles on the road, and they were all headed in the same direction. James fell in line.

They heard the commotion before they saw anything. It sounded like a hundred people were blowing their horns. Emily rolled down her window so she could hear better. Then she rolled it back up. The obnoxiousness of the noise overpowered her curiosity.

James pulled the truck in behind a long string of parked vehicles and shut off the engine.

"Where are we?" Emily asked.

"Not sure, but it sounds like the action is at Travis Payne's place." He started walking along the slim shoulder, and Emily had to double-time it to keep up with his long legs.

"Thomas's house?"

"Well, I doubt he pays the mortgage, but yes."

The backside of a lovely Dutch Colonial came into view. The front of the house faced the ocean, and Thomas and his family enjoyed a spectacular view of the harbor.

"Wow," Emily said. "I'm glad *I* don't have to pay the mortgage either."

"No kidding."

"Seriously though, what *is* that noise?" They had started down the driveway, toward a crowd of people.

James started to laugh.

"What?" she said, looking up at him in the darkness. She had to speak loudly to drown out the horns.

"I think they are air horns."

"What?" she said, even louder, now that they'd gotten closer. Then she saw it. Sure enough, there were about twenty people standing immediately behind Thomas's house, each holding a portable air horn. Some of them held one in each hand. Every air horn was blatting, creating a synergistic effect that made Emily want to die. She had the urge to cover her ears, but no one else was doing that, and she wanted to appear tough too.

Sheriff Pease was trying to break up the crowd, but wasn't having much luck. He now stood in front of the troublemakers and was hollering in their faces, but it appeared that they were all ignoring him. Emily wondered how many pairs of handcuffs he had. She also wondered why on earth they were doing what they were doing.

She saw that James was chuckling. She couldn't hear him, but he was smiling and his chest was shaking. She looked at him quizzically.

He muttered something.

"What?" Emily hollered.

"They're making noise," James hollered.

"Yeah, I gathered that much," Emily hollered back.

James looked down at her, and she noticed he was incredibly handsome in the moonlight. "Windmills make noise," he hollered. "So they're making noise."

Chapter 16

When James picked Emily up the next morning, she noticed two things: one) he smelled like cinnamonic heaven; and two) he looked annoyed.

"What's wrong?" she asked as he pulled out onto the main road.

"This is already getting out of hand."

"What? The windmills? I thought you thought the air horns were hysterical."

"Well, they were, kind of, unless they do it again. Or unless they do it in front of my house. Look." He pointed to her right.

She looked. A giant cardboard sign read: SAY NO TO WIND.

"Oh dear," Emily said.

A hundred yards beyond that: SAVE OUR ISLAND. And then: SAVE THE BIRDS.

She couldn't help it. She started to giggle.

"I know. It's kind of funny," James admitted. "But I have a feeling we're on the edge of something and if we go over the edge, it won't be funny anymore."

The next sign read only INFRASOUND but the word was circled in red paint and a red line was drawn diagonally down through the word. Then the sign was put up before it had completely dried, so the red slash was dripping down the sign, making it look eerily like blood. Emily wondered if this effect had been accidental.

"Yeah," she said, "I see your point." The signs were on both sides of the road, all the way into town. "People have been busy. Who has this much time?" she wondered aloud.

"Jane Crockett."

"Really?"

"Yeah, I think that woman was just sitting around waiting for a cause."

"So she was probably behind the air horn protest?"

"They're calling it a 'sound demonstration' and yes, she was."

"Who told you that?"

"I never reveal my sources," he said with a half-smile that made her stomach flip. She thought back to the first time she had seen him, on the ferry, on her way to the island, how handsome she had thought he was. But now, it seemed every time she saw him, he grew more handsome. She wondered if he would keep growing handsome—would she wake up after twenty years of marriage and think he was even more handsome than the day before? That pleasant feeling in her stomach morphed into anxiety as she wondered why he hadn't proposed yet, when he was going to propose, *was* he going to propose, had he changed his mind, and she silently prayed that God would take that anxiousness from her.

Abe and Lily's basement, which Emily couldn't help but think of as Noah's basement, was crowded as usual. Their band of believers grew every week. The little congregation wasn't so little anymore.

It seemed the windmill drama didn't follow the islanders down the stairs—at first. Abe welcomed everyone and then prayed. He prayed for God to be mightily present for their worship, he prayed for Ellie Newman who had just been diagnosed with cancer, and then he asked God to interrupt the windmill plans.

Emily suppressed a gasp and then listened intently to try to ascertain if anyone else in the room was gasping. But the room remained silent. She resisted the urge to look up, but as soon as Abe said amen, she succumbed to her urge and looked around the room. And many a face looked disgusted. Abe, seemingly unaware of his bold provocation, began to invite someone up to give that morning's message, but he was interrupted by Heather Ginn, MacKenzie's mom.

"Just a second, Abe. I'm not sure we should be asking God to stop the windmills, when most of us in here are *for* the windmills." This brought several argumentative grunts. Maybe "most of us" was an exaggeration. Heather, either not hearing the grunts or choosing to ignore them, continued, "God made the wind, so shouldn't we use it?"

The grunts evolved into groans. Someone said, "Spare us the hippie talk, Heather. This island has done just fine for centuries—"

"Wait!" Abe cried. "I'm sorry, I didn't mean to start an argument. I apologize for my prayer. I was praying my own wants, forgetting that I was speaking for all of us—"

"Well, I think we *should* discuss it," someone said.

"We *can*," Abe said, "*after* the service. Right now, I ask you all to join me in prayer again." Without giving anyone a chance to argue, Abe bowed his head, closed his eyes, and cleared his throat. "Father, forgive me. Forgive me for bringing my agenda into your meeting. Forgive me for making assumptions. I ask you to help us focus on you, on worshipping you. And I ask you to help us live and love like brothers and sisters, even when we disagree. In your precious son's name, amen." He looked up, nodded to the man who was to give the message, and then quickly sat down.

Emily looked at James wide-eyed, and James raised an eyebrow that said, "See? I told you."

Chapter 17

On Monday morning, Emily felt like a little kid on Christmas. She was almost embarrassed about how excited she was to start softball. James and she had gone to the mainland after church to buy softballs—she'd sprung for these—and she had placed an order online for all the other equipment. On her way to her classroom, she stopped into the office to hand Julie an announcement and then practically ran out of the office to avoid Julie's commentary. She still heard it.

"She expects me to read *this*?" Julie said to the empty office.

So Emily wasn't really surprised when Julie *didn't* include her notice in the morning announcements. Not surprised. But still furious. People announced ridiculous stuff all the time—if Julie could announce the special ed teacher's lunchtime scented wax sale, then surely she could announce *this*. Emily asked the librarian to cover her room and then made a beeline for the office, hoping Julie wouldn't be at her desk. She was, but Emily decided she didn't care. She grabbed the microphone and flipped the on switch before Julie could protest. Then, though Julie tried to grab the mic out of her hands, Emily said, "Sorry for the interruption. We forgot one of our morning announcements. Softball pitchers and catchers will start today in the gym at four. Please wear sneakers and bring your gloves if you have them. And the Piercehaven softball team would like to give a special thank you to Travis Payne, who generously donated the funds necessary to make this softball team happen."

She gave Julie a smile that she knew was evilly smug, and set the microphone down with exaggerated care.

"You are so lucky Mr. Hogan isn't here," Julie said through gritted teeth.

Emily didn't know how to respond to that, so she just walked away with an uneasy feeling in her gut. She knew this was a pattern with her. Occasionally, she would be filled with an almost supernatural bravery and she would do something she thought wonderful, but then soon after, she would be overcome with dread of the consequences. Hurrying back up the hallway to her room, she tried to push the dread out, telling herself she'd done a good thing, but then Kyle stepped out of his classroom.

"You never cease to surprise me."

She smiled and continued.

"Don't say I didn't try to warn you," he said to her back.

Victoria beamed at Emily when she walked back into her classroom. "We really got all the stuff?"

Emily thanked the librarian and then flashed Victoria a smile she no longer felt. "Yes, Mr. Payne bought us everything, and Noah, Noah's father, and Mr. Gagnon fixed up your field. So we are good to go."

"That musta cost Travis a bundle," Victoria said.

"Don't worry," Tyler said, "he can afford it."

At four o'clock sharp, there were five girls and two surprises in the gym. The first surprise: Alongside stalwarts Hailey, Chloe, MacKenzie, and Ava, stood Juniper. The second surprise: Beside Juniper, stood Thomas.

"You know managers don't have to come to practice?" Emily said to him.

"You kidding? I wouldn't miss this."

Emily looked at those present. "Where is everyone else?"

Juniper rolled her eyes. Hailey answered, "A lot of them are still in the locker room."

Emily was annoyed. "Why? I'm guessing they're never late for basketball practice?"

Hailey shrugged. "This isn't basketball, Miss M."

"I could go get them," Thomas said. He was trying to be funny. No one laughed, and Chloe elbowed him in the ribs.

Emily headed for the locker room and met two more girls on the way out. "You're late," she said, and they looked chagrined. She stormed the door like a gunslinger entering a saloon. "What are you guys doing?"

They appeared to be doing very little. Hannah was tying her shoe and everyone else was watching her. Hannah looked up. "We're coming, we're coming, *geesh*."

Emily waited for them to exit before she followed them out. Then she approached her gaggle, the sight of which cheered her. This was her team. Her team and Thomas. "OK, guys. I'm so, so glad you're here. But one thing: I'm not going to scream at you and make you run for being late, but I am going to ask you to respect your teammates and me enough to show up on time. OK?"

Most of them nodded. Emily noticed that DeAnna was missing. "Anyone seen DeAnna?"

"I don't think she's going to play, Miss M," Hannah said.

"Did she tell you that?"

"No, but she's never played a sport in her life."

"OK then. Let's get warmed up." Emily took them through a series of dynamic stretching that she had found on YouTube only a few hours prior. Once they'd done that, she asked them to partner up and play pass.

And then Emily's pie in the sky fell to the floor with a splat.

Three girls didn't even have gloves, but it didn't matter because softballs were flying everywhere except *into* the softball gloves. Emily had never seen such a mess. Scarcely three weeks ago these girls had been athletic prodigies; now they looked like ungainly scarecrows flopping their limbs around. She couldn't imagine what Juniper must be thinking. *Someone is going to get hurt.* "Wait!" she cried. They stopped and looked at her expectantly, and her horror tempered a bit. She took a deep breath. "I apologize. I should have given more specific instructions. MacKenzie, Chloe, Juniper, Jasmine, Sydney,

Ava, Hailey, and Sara, you stand on this line." She put her foot on the sideline. They followed her instructions. "Now put about four feet between each of you." They spread out. Then she walked about ten feet away from them. "Now the rest of you line up here"—she pointed—"across from them, so that all of our balls are going in the same direction," she said. "Approximately," she added.

They all stood looking at her. "OK. Go ahead. Throw."

They threw. And immediately the gym filled with the loathsome sound of balls banging into folded up wooden bleachers. A softball hit senior Allie Cousens square in the chest. She swore. Emily thought Allie hadn't played a sport before and chose to pretend she didn't hear the curse. "OK, everyone, we're just getting started, so just throw the ball nice and easy." She could practically hear Juniper's eyes roll at that one. She did hear Thomas laugh.

She made her way down the line, dodging a couple of stray fires and found MacKenzie calmly catching and throwing the ball. *Thank you, Father.* "Lookin' good, MacKenzie."

MacKenzie gave her a half-smile that quickly faded. "You regretting this yet?"

Emily stepped closer to her. "Regretting what?"

"Starting a softball team!" MacKenzie said quietly, but with feeling. "We're pretty terrible."

"We all have to start somewhere, and we're going to be fine. But you're a little correct. I didn't expect such a rough start. Didn't these girls play pass in the yard with their dads growing up?"

MacKenzie snorted. "Yeah. With a basketball."

Emily couldn't help it. She laughed at this as she made her way down the line. Of course, Juniper looked amazing. Hailey didn't look terrible. But after that, it was a somber state of affairs. Chloe looked a little like a seagull.

"Hey!" someone screamed from the doorway. Emily didn't need to turn around to know it was Larry. But she turned anyway. So did all the girls. "You going to pay for all this damage?" Larry shouted.

Emily looked around, afraid she had missed a window breaking or something, but Larry didn't give her a chance to decipher his ambiguity. "Those bleachers are fifty years old!"

Emily didn't know what to say. A few of the girls giggled. "Thank you," Emily managed, "we'll be more careful."

"You better be!" Larry shouted. He sounded completely unhinged. "Or we can put a stop to this whole softball nonsense!" And he vanished, leaving Emily to wonder how on earth the custodian could put a stop to an athletic team. The scary part was, Emily thought he probably could.

"Come here, guys," Emily said, trying to appear cool and collected, when she felt shaky and near tears. The girls gathered round. "Please ignore that. It is completely normal for people to miss balls on the first day. But I'm going to make a small change so we make less noise for Larry. Hailey, would you please take Jasmine, Lucy, and Allie to that corner over there and go over the basic mechanics of throwing. MacKenzie, please do the same in that corner with Sydney, Victoria, and Sara. And would the rest of you please stay here with Juniper."

Everyone obeyed. Juniper looked at her over the top of the glove she was chewing on. "You want me to teach these girls how to throw?" she said.

"Not teach them," Emily tried. "Just help them to refine their technique."

"Why can't you teach them to throw?" Juniper said. "Aren't you the coach?"

Emily fought to keep her voice under control as she said, "Juniper, go over to the corner there and have a seat."

Juniper looked at the empty corner and then looked at her, appalled. "You're telling me to go sit in the corner? What am I, five?"

Emily took a step toward her. "I'm telling you to either go sit in a time out or get out of my gym."

Juniper stood there for a few seconds, seeming to gauge her sincerity, and then went and sat in the corner. Emily waited until she had done so and then turned to the small group and asked for a ball. Ava handed her one. And then Emily showed them how to throw a ball.

Chapter 18

After a half-hour of practicing throwing overhand, there was significantly less banging. Juniper sat with her back against the wall, arms crossed and eyes blazing. Emily approached her. "I would like to invite you to rejoin us now, but I'm serious, Juniper—I can't allow you to disrespect me like that."

"Disrespect?" Juniper whined indignantly. "How about making me sit in the corner—how's that for disrespect? Are you kidding me? I should quit this stupid team. You're not going to win a game without me."

Emily squatted down to be eye level with her. "Juniper, I would rather lose every game than give in to your stubborn, childish antics. So if you want to quit, quit. If you want to stay, then act like an athlete." She stayed perched there, looking at her for a few seconds, and then she stood and walked away.

After a moment, she heard Juniper get up and follow her.

"Come on, guys," Emily said. "Bring it in." Most of them trotted toward her. A few lollygagged, but she let them. She started talking before they all got there. "Now I'm starting at the very beginning because this is our first year. I know that most of you know most of this, so don't be offended by how simple I'm trying to make it." She took a big breath. "In softball, pitchers pitch the ball underhand." She glanced at Juniper who *didn't* roll her eyes at this. Emily was greatly encouraged. "You've all probably seen softball pitchers windmill the ball"—she demonstrated in slow-mo—"but you absolutely *don't* have to windmill pitch." She paused, waiting for the argument.

Hailey provided it. "Isn't every other team going to windmill?"

"I have no idea," Emily admitted.

"Rangeley's pitcher doesn't windmill," Natalie said.

"You've got to be kidding," Juniper said.

"How do you know that?" Hailey asked.

Natalie shrugged. "Someone told me."

"Who on earth do you know in Rangeley?" Hailey asked.

Natalie blushed, making everyone think her mystery friend was a boy. "I mean, I don't think they are very good, but they don't have a windmiller."

"That's Class D for you," Juniper muttered.

"Oh, and what class was your last school, Miss Big Deal?" Sydney said.

"Class A Southern Maine Champs," Juniper said. "You got anything else you want to say?"

Sydney opened her mouth to say more.

"Sydney!" Emily scolded.

"Me?" Sydney cried defensively.

"The point is," Emily said, "I can teach any of you to windmill if you're interested. But whether or not you're interested, *someone* is going to have to pitch, and I don't yet know who that will be. So we're all going to try at least a basic underhand pitch."

"But we have Juniper," Jasmine said.

Emily looked at Juniper. "Yes, we do. But we're going to need more than one pitcher."

"Why?" Jasmine asked.

Because we can't count on her—at all. And even if we could, people get sick. People get injured. "Because we will. Just trust me. OK, we're not actually going to get into a catcher's position until we get some protective gear, but for now, Juniper, would you please go stand in front of the wall pads?"

Juniper looked at her as if she'd asked for a kidney. Emily quickly walked over to her. "I just need someone who can actually catch the balls. I'm not asking you to be a catcher. Just humor me, OK?"

Her expression transformed from irritated to acquiescent as she realized the common sense of Emily's request, and she jogged to the end of the gym.

"All right, now the rest of you"—Emily paced off forty feet—"line up here."

A small squabble ensued, as no one wanted to be first, and finally MacKenzie took the spot. Emily set the bucket of balls at her feet. "OK, MacKenzie. Absolutely no pressure. Just do your best. Try to hit the glove."

MacKenzie looked as though she felt no pressure whatsoever. She might have been flying a kite at the beach. She flung her arm back, bent over, and fired the ball to Juniper.

And it almost got there. It hit the floor with a distinct lack of oomph and then rolled to Juniper, who bent over, grabbed it, then stood and quickly returned it to MacKenzie. The first six girls in line all ducked as though it were a missile set to explode on impact, but MacKenzie caught it.

"Sorry," Juniper mumbled.

MacKenzie looked at Emily.

"Again."

MacKenzie threw the ball again. This time it made it to Juniper, but barely.

"Again."

MacKenzie looked at her as if to ask, "Really?"

"Really," Emily said.

MacKenzie pitched the ball again and though it didn't travel fast, it took a completely straight path and landed square in Juniper's glove.

"Not bad," Juniper said, and Emily almost fell down in shock. Not so much at the pitch, which was a surprise, but at the fact that Juniper had uttered two encouraging syllables.

"Next," Emily said, trying to look impassive. James had rubbed off on her—a little.

Hailey stepped up looking as though she were about to throw a pitch in a state championship extra inning.

"Just relax, Hailey."

Hailey showed no signs of relaxing. She flung her arm back and threw the ball, apparently as hard as she could, toward Juniper. It went about three feet wide to the right. Hailey and Juniper swore in unison.

"Girls," Emily scolded.

Juniper chased the ball down, again surprising Emily, and fired it back to Hailey, who didn't catch it. Hailey chased it all the way to the other end of the gym and then ran back to her spot. "Can I try again?"

"Of course."

Her second pitch went wild to the left. Her face grew red and her fist clenched. Emily walked over to her. "Hailey, just relax. Don't try to throw it so hard. Just throw it."

Apparently Hailey misunderstood because this time she lobbed the ball toward Juniper and it floated for an eternity before dropping into the strike zone from above. Emily figured this was better than nothing and said, "Next."

Chloe threw it over Juniper's head three times in a row.

Jasmine let go of the ball during her windup, and it hit Sydney, who was standing six feet behind her.

Sara couldn't get the ball to travel forty feet. Neither could Allie.

Hannah rolled one and hit the basketball backboard with another.

Sydney spent at least an hour on her windup and then was furious when it rolled forty feet. She tried again, didn't shorten up her windup despite being encouraged to do so, and didn't improve on her pitch. Emily didn't let her try a third time.

Lucy, Natalie, and Victoria refused to try at all.

WINDMILLS

Ava threw it straight and true, two out of three times.

Kylie Greem, seventh grader, asked if she could windmill, was told not yet, sulked a little, and threw three strikes in a row.

Emily made a mental note: Hailey, Ava, and a seventh grader were their only hopes. And she wasn't sure it was even safe to put a seventh grader on the mound. She guessed Richmond could probably hit the ball—hard.

Chapter 19

"Great job, guys. I mean it," Emily said. "Same time and place tomorrow. I'm going to let you go early, but if you have to wait for a ride, obviously stay right here. Juniper and MacKenzie, I'm going to ask you to stay a while longer."

She waited for the rest of the team to saunter off; then she turned her attention to her only real pitcher. "OK, Juniper. I don't want to ask MacKenzie to catch for you until she gets her gear on—"

"You know she's like *really* small for a catcher, right?"

Emily thought she knew then what a mother bear feels like just before she rips a predator's head off. "Juniper, you know absolutely nothing about this athlete. And the day will come, *if* you pitch for us, when you will be thanking me that she's the catcher. Also, don't interrupt me when I'm talking. Now, as I was saying, I would like to see your warmup routine, so let's go through it with MacKenzie. But don't throw full speed at her. Understand?"

Juniper's lips were tight and her cheeks were red, but she nodded.

"OK then. Let's warm you up."

Juniper stood only three feet away from MacKenzie and flicked the ball at her—hard. It didn't appear that MacKenzie knew it was coming or that it was going to come at her that fast. She caught it, clumsily, and tossed it back. Emily watched MacKenzie's face, and she didn't look annoyed—just incredibly focused—so Emily stayed out of it. She walked away and leaned back on the bleachers, hoping against hope that if she gave them some space, they might bond—a little. Emily saw that Jake Jasper had appeared, and now stood leaning against the wall, his arms crossed, watching his daughter. Emily looked at the clock, but they still had fifteen minutes.

Juniper and MacKenzie fell into an efficient rhythm. Snap, slap, return. Snap, slap, return. Clockwork. Emily couldn't believe how well MacKenzie was catching the ball. Though Juniper wasn't throwing the ball at full speed yet, it was still traveling at a pretty swift clip.

Juniper stepped back, looked at Emily and said, "This is usually where I start to throw hard."

"OK, thank you, Juniper," Emily said, walking toward them. "The second we get the equipment, I'll let you throw full speed."

"Can my dad just catch for me?"

Emily didn't know how to respond.

"I can do it, Miss M," MacKenzie insisted, as Jake started across the gym.

"Please?" Juniper said, "I want to show you."

Emily looked at Jake.

"I'm happy to," Jake said, and he did look happy. Thrilled even. "Can I borrow your glove?" he asked MacKenzie.

She took it off and gave it to him, but she looked absolutely disgusted about it. "I can catch," MacKenzie said, "but Miss M won't let me because we don't have *equipment* yet."

"Your coach is absolutely right," Jake said. "Juniper throws hard, and you don't want to get hurt the first day."

"I can catch the ball," MacKenzie insisted, folding her arms across her chest.

Jake gave her a big smile, and then as he walked away, said, "I'm sure you can, kiddo, but she doesn't always throw strikes, and if that ball bounces, there's no telling where it's going to come up." He squatted down and looked at his daughter. "OK, let 'er rip, kid."

MacKenzie and Emily stepped back to watch.

Juniper squared up, shook out her arms, went through a simple windup and then she *let her rip*.

"Holy cannoli," MacKenzie said under her breath.

Emily's jaw dropped. She had known Juniper would have speed, but she had no idea she would throw like *that*.

Jake caught the fastball strike and threw it back to his daughter without coming out of his squat. She wound up and did it again. Emily was no expert on windmilling, but her form looked textbook, and the ball—well, the pitch was a thing of beauty. Straight down the middle, no rising or dropping, and *fast*. *No one in this league is going to be able to hit that*, she thought.

For the first time, Emily felt a niggling sense of competitiveness. *Maybe we could win a game this year. Maybe we could win more than one.*

Chapter 20

James entered the gym just as Juniper threw her last pitch. Emily praised Juniper a little, MacKenzie a lot, and then thanked Jake profusely for catching for his daughter. Without saying so, she was also thanking him for bringing his ringer to her island. Then she approached James.

"Hi, James. What are you doing here?"

"What was that all about?" he asked, sounding grumpy.

"What?" She looked behind her as if the answer lay in the now empty gym.

"Who was that guy?"

"Oh, that's Juniper's father."

"The windmill guy?"

Emily frowned. "You're starting to sound anti-windmill. But yes, he's a foreman … or something. James, what's wrong?"

"And he's practicing with you? Do you really think that's appropriate?"

Emily held both hands up. "Whoa, James. He didn't *practice* with us. He just showed up at the end, you know, to *pick up* his daughter. We don't have any catcher's equipment yet, so I wasn't letting MacKenzie catch for Juniper. So he offered. Juniper wanted to show me her stuff, and he caught a few pitches for her. That's all."

James's jaw clenched. "Well, you might want to be careful. There are people on this island who wouldn't like that."

"James, *you* sound like one of those people. What's your problem?"

"What's my problem? I drop in to check on my future wife 'cause she's doing something *crazy* again, and I find her hanging out in an almost empty gym with some single windmill foreman."

Before he even finished his sentence, Emily took two quick steps and wrapped her arms around him. She didn't even hear the second half of what he said. If she had, she might've wondered how James knew that Jake Jasper the windmill guy was single, but if she'd wondered, she would've just admitted that island people just know things, that personal information seems to travel on the sea's breezes. But she didn't care about any of that, because James had called her his "future wife." That meant all systems were a go. He still wanted to marry her. A proper proposal was still forthcoming. Maybe Thomas had been right. Maybe they were just waiting on a ring.

Emily walked into school on Tuesday morning with a bounce in her step. She had a pitcher from heaven and a husband in store. Could life get any better?

During second period, Hailey asked if she could talk to Emily after class. Emily said of course. Hailey had been uncharacteristically quiet during class and Emily wondered if softball was the root.

"What's up?" Emily asked when Hailey's classmates had vacated the room.

"I was just wondering if I'm going to pitch at all."

Emily suppressed a chuckle. "Do you *want* to pitch?"

Hailey shrugged. It looked like false humility.

"No, really. Are you asking because you want to pitch and you're worried you're not going to get to, or because you *don't* want to pitch and you're worried you're going to have to?"

"I obviously know I'm not going to *have* to pitch. We've got Juniper, and she's like amazing or whatever. MacKenzie told me. But I still would like to try."

"Well, then of course you can try. And I haven't said anything about who is pitching when. We've only had one practice. If you want to pitch, then keep working at it. I have no idea what's going to—"

"But Miss M, that's my point. I don't *want* to work at it if there's no point to it, if Juniper is just going to pitch all season."

Emily leaned forward in her chair and looked up at the serious young woman. "Hailey, you of all people know that's not the way a sports team works. I honestly don't know yet if we will need you to pitch. As I was saying before you interrupted me, I don't know what's going to happen today, let alone four, six, or eight weeks from now. Now, do I think it would be a good idea if you would practice pitching a bit, just in case? Yes. Of course. But am I going to *make* you practice? No, I am not." Emily heard pounding on the classroom door. Period three was ready to come in. She ignored them. "And there's more to a softball team than its pitcher, Hailey. Juniper might keep them from hitting the ball, but she can't score runs from the pitcher's mound. We're also going to have to

136

get on base. And we're going to have to run the bases. So whether you pitch or not, we need you—you know that, right?"

Hailey nodded, looking satiated.

"Great. Now, would you please go let my AP students in? It's time for class."

At lunchtime, Emily tried to act casually as she approached DeAnna's mostly empty table. Juniper sat at the other end of the table, and Blake sat opposite her. He gave Emily a critical look as she slid into the seat opposite DeAnna. *He probably thinks I'm interfering with his courting*, she thought, and then silently made fun of herself for calling it courting.

"Hi, DeAnna," she said, trying to sound perky.

"Hi."

"We missed you at softball practice yesterday."

"I said I wasn't going to play."

"I know. But I really want you to. So what's it going to take?"

DeAnna stared at her. "Why do you care?"

Emily shrugged. Now was probably not the time to tell DeAnna that she cared because Jesus cared. "I just do. So, will you play?"

"I don't have a glove."

"We can get you one," Emily said quickly.

"I don't have any sneakers."

"We can get you some of those too."

DeAnna stared again. "OK."

"OK?" Emily was surprised.

"OK. You know I'm going to suck, right?"

"It's not about that. It's about getting outside, getting some exercise, and being part of a team."

"Miss Morse, no one on that team wants me to be part of their team."

Something in Emily's heart cracked. "I don't think that's true, DeAnna, and even if it is, so what? I want you to be part of the team."

DeAnna didn't look convinced. "Bojack says you just want me on the team because you want a team and there's not enough girls."

It took Emily a second to remember who Bojack was, and when she did, she wondered why he would be talking to DeAnna about softball. "First of all, we have more than enough girls signed up. And second of all, how do you know Bojack?"

DeAnna scrunched her brow together. "This is Piercehaven. Everyone knows everyone."

"I know that, but why do you know him well enough to listen to his advice about softball? Is he your uncle or something?"

"Ew! No!" DeAnna said, as if that were absurd. "He's my mom's boyfriend."

"Oh!" Emily said, careful to hide her cringe. "I didn't know that. How long have they been dating?"

"Couple a months, but I wouldn't call it dating. He just sits on our couch and drinks beer. And he's technically still married to someone else."

"Sorry to hear that. Sounds like yet another reason to spend some time away from home."

DeAnna looked confused.

"You know, if you're on the softball field, you'll get a break from your mom's boyfriend."

DeAnna actually smiled.

Chapter 21

All the girls showed up on time to the second pitchers and catchers practice. Even DeAnna. Also Thomas. Emily's heart was warmed at the sight. "Hailey, do you remember the stretches we went through yesterday?"

"Yep."

"Could you lead your teammates through them again?"

"Yep." She headed toward the sideline, and her teammates followed, except for DeAnna.

"Did you get my sneakers yet?" DeAnna asked expectantly.

Emily chuckled. "DeAnna, I promised you sneakers at lunchtime. How could I have possibly gotten them yet?"

DeAnna shrugged. "Well, I can't do anything without them."

Emily looked down at her feet. She was wearing a pair of weathered Converse high tops. Emily looked at her face again. "First of all, when you said you didn't have sneakers, I thought you meant cleats, which is what we'll all be wearing when we get outside, and we *will* be getting outside soon. I will help you find cleats. But for now, those will do."

"But I don't have a glove."

Emily looked at the rest of the girls, who were now a third of the way through warmups. "You don't need a glove to stretch out. Now go join your team."

DeAnna's eyes grew wide. "You made me join this team and now you're being rude!" Then she stomped off toward the rest of the girls, leaving Emily to wonder if the child knew the definition of the word *rude*.

After stretches, Emily asked those with gloves to line up in pairs to throw overhand. "In a minute, we'll switch out and some of you can lend your gloves to those who don't have them yet." They began to throw, but there was a noticeable lag in chitchat. Emily took this to mean they were concentrating. She was wrong. They were conspiring.

Chloe approached her. "Um, Miss M? The girls don't want to share their gloves."

"What? Why?"

"Um, because it's kind of gross."

Emily didn't know what to say to that. She didn't think it was gross, but she also couldn't *make* anyone share her glove. "Are you telling me that you, Chloe, are not going to share your glove with a teammate?"

Chloe looked guilty. "If I do it, then the other girls will get mad and feel like they should."

"They *should*."

Chloe looked guiltier. "Please don't make me, Miss M."

"I'm not going to *make* you, but I *am* disappointed—"

"You have to understand, Miss M. It's not everyone. It's just …" Her voice trailed off.

"It's just what?"

"Not what. *Who*. It's just that no one wants to share with DeAnna."

"What? Well, that's incredibly unkind of you. Just because you're not friends with someone—"

"It's not that, Miss M. It's that … well"—she lowered her voice even more—"she's just … *dirty*."

A vision of Stephen King's Carrie flashed through Emily's mind, which made her even angrier than she would have been. "That's enough. I don't want to hear another word," Emily said through an almost closed jaw." Then she raised her voice to everyone. "I've changed my mind! We're going to do things a little differently—"

Juniper had sprinted over to her, so she stopped talking. "They can use my glove. Just rotate them all through it. It's not like I need to practice throwing."

"Really?" Emily said.

Juniper gave Chloe a disgusted look. "Yeah, really." Then she trotted over to DeAnna and handed her glove over.

"Never mind," Emily said loudly. "It seems we have a plan. Carry on." She looked at her precious Chloe. "Get back in line."

"Miss M, I'm sorry, but please try—"

"Just go throw, Chloe. I'm not angry. Just go throw." Chloe left, her head down and her shoulders slumped. Emily wasn't angry, not really. But she did hold Chloe to a higher standard, because Chloe professed Christ, so she should know better. But immediately on the heels of this expectation came Emily's own guilt. Chloe was still just a kid, Jesus or no Jesus, and she was still learning. And there was no doubt that someone else had sent her to Emily as the team's spokesperson.

"What was that all about?" Thomas said. He had approached from behind.

"We have four girls without gloves. The girls with gloves didn't want to share. So I was going to make them do something else, but then Juniper offered to share her glove." As

Emily spoke, Juniper was helping DeAnna with her throwing form. *What an unpredictable child.*

"So what you're saying is, Juniper's the hero?"

Emily thought she heard a touch of admiration in his voice. "I don't know about that. But she's doing a kind thing, for sure."

After they'd thrown for a while, Emily sent MacKenzie and Juniper down to one end of the gym and lined everyone else up as they'd done the day before, with Hailey back-to to the gym pads.

Again, it wasn't pretty. But this time they went through the line several times and at least the girls began to relax. At first Hailey did a lot of chasing as the pitched balls sometimes landed nowhere near her, but then Thomas took over that duty, leaving Hailey to catch only the balls in her immediate vicinity, which allowed for far more pitches. Emily thought perhaps it would be better to have one of her athletes chase the balls down, but Thomas seemed to be having so much fun.

After a while, Emily switched Hailey out with Ava, who actually did a better job of catching the ball than Hailey had. "Nice job, Ava! Are you sure you've never played softball before?"

Ava beamed at the praise. "No, but I used to play Little League."

"Really? I bet you were adorable."

"I don't know about that. But I loved it. Was pretty bummed when I got too old to play."

Ava was a senior. Seemed the Piercehaven softball team had formed in the nick of time.

Chapter 22

When Emily entered her classroom on Friday morning, Thomas quickly said, "Shut the door!"

Emily did. "Why?"

"Because there's too much drama out there," Thomas said.

"Because Thomas is afraid of DeAnna," Chloe said.

"What? Why?"

"I'm not *afraid* of her," Thomas said, ignoring Emily's questions. "I just don't want to deal with her."

"Why?" Emily repeated.

"She had a few choice words for Thomas this morning," Chloe said. "But only because she overheard him saying some stupid stuff of his own."

"What did you say?" Emily asked.

"I was just talking to Blake in the hallway and I said something about Bojack. I was just kidding. But DeAnna overheard me and freaked out."

"DeAnna defended Bojack?" Emily found that hard to believe.

"Yeah, well he's like her father or something," Thomas said with thick distaste.

"No, he's not. He's only been dating her mom a few months," Emily said.

Thomas and Chloe looked at her, surprised, and Thomas said, "Look at you, official island know-it-all. Whatever. My point is, he lives with her, and so she's mad."

It was Emily's turn to be surprised. "He *lives* with her? I didn't know that." She finally sat down. "I am so confused. Will you please start at the beginning and tell me what you said?"

Thomas looked at Chloe.

"He doesn't want to," Chloe explained. "It was pretty mean."

"And it was also supposed to be private. I was just talking to Blake."

"You were not," Chloe said. "There were like five other guys standing around and you said it loud enough for them all to hear. You were trying to get a laugh. And you got it, but DeAnna heard it too."

"Just tell me!" Emily said. Her impatience was overwhelming her.

Thomas took a deep breath. "OK, but don't hate me? You love me, but you know I can be a jerk sometimes, right?"

"Just tell me!" Emily said again.

"OK, so I was just kidding. I said that Bojack probably doesn't mind being in jail because it's nicer than his house."

Emily stared at him as she processed this. The cruelty of his comment didn't surprise her at all. What surprised her was the word jail, and the phrase "his house." "You mean, DeAnna's house?"

"Well, yeah," Thomas stammered, "but he lives there. It would have been extra mean to say 'nicer than DeAnna's house.'"

"No, I'm not suggesting that you should have been more specific. I'm just trying to point out that DeAnna was probably defending her *house*, not her mother's unpleasant boyfriend."

Thomas shrugged. "Maybe, but then she started freaking out about how it's my dad's fault that Bojack's in jail and that the whole island knows that, and my dad's a creep, blah, blah, blah."

Emily frowned. "Your dad put Bojack in jail?"

Thomas looked incredulous. "Haven't you heard about what happened last night?"

"Obviously not!" Emily said, defensive. "I get all my island news from you two!"

Thomas laughed. "OK," he began, shifting forward in his chair as if he couldn't wait to deliver something savory, "last night Bojack got in a fistfight with some windmill guy—"

"Jake?"

"No, not Jake," Thomas said, looking peeved at the interruption, "someone else, someone who just got here. They were both hammered, and they went outside and beat the snot out of each other. The sheriff finally came and put Bojack in jail."

"Didn't he get medical attention first? And what jail? We don't have a jail? And why just Bojack? What about the other guy?"

Thomas put both his hands up to stop the barrage of questions. "Slow down! I don't know, or care, about his medical attention, but they took him off on the first ferry this morning to the jail in Rockland, and he got arrested because he had a knife. He actually cut the guy."

Emily's eyes grew wide. This had gone from juicy gossip to scary news.

"He's OK," Thomas hurried to comfort her, "people broke it up, but still, assault with a weapon and all that. Bojack could go to prison. Again."

Emily let out a slow breath. "No wonder DeAnna's upset."

Thomas made a pfft sound. "Not like he helps with the bills or anything. The guy's a slug. DeAnna's mom's just desperate."

"Thomas, I fear this situation is bringing out the worst in you."

Thomas sat up a little straighter and squared his shoulders. "Maybe, but I'm sick of an entire island full of white trash crapping all over my father just for being a businessman. And Bojack doesn't care about the stupid windmills, even if he does live right beside them. He's just looking for a reason to fight."

"Right beside them? Where does DeAnna live?"

Thomas looked positively haughty as he said, "In a broken down trailer on top of Chicken Hill."

Julie called Emily out of her third period class. Emily asked the librarian to cover for her, and then headed down the hall. As she got closer to the office, she saw a giant pile of cardboard boxes. "Yes?" She stuck her head into the office.

"Would you please get that stuff out of my hallway?" Julie snapped.

Emily looked at the boxes, but it took several seconds for it to click that those were *her* boxes. Then her heart leapt with excitement.

"Now?" Julie pressed.

Emily looked at her. The woman's unpleasantness still surprised her after almost an entire school year. "You know I have a class right now, right? Couldn't this have waited until—"

"You know people have to use that hallway, right?"

Emily turned the other cheek and moved the boxes, one by one, into the girls' locker room. She was notably tempted to rip into them right then and there, but she *did* have a class she was supposed to be educating, no matter what the school secretary said.

When the girls saw the bats at practice, they went crazy. Emily had unboxed everything and put the bats into the bat bag, and the girls scrambled to get them out of the bag, as if it were Christmas and there were only five presents for fifteen girls. DeAnna and Juniper stood out of the fray—DeAnna didn't seem to care, and Juniper had seen bats before. Emily eyed them—together but not together. They stood nowhere near each other, yet seemed to share the bond of being outcasts.

"That's enough," she said, trying to sound firm. "We're not allowed to touch bats this week. On Monday, we'll start batting."

"Do we even have a batting cage?" Juniper asked, her nose pointed at the ceiling.

Emily didn't know, so she ignored the question.

"The boys do," Hailey said. "I bet they'll let us use it."

"I wouldn't bet on anything," Ava said. "The pitching machine is for baseball, and Larry's the one who sets it up, and I'm pretty sure he's not going to do anything to help the softball team."

"Who's Larry?" Juniper asked.

"The janitor," Thomas said with disdain.

"Why won't he set up the pitching machine for softball? Isn't that his job?" Juniper asked.

Several of the girls, and Thomas, laughed at this.

"Larry is the janitor, but he thinks he's the mayor," Thomas said.

"Larry hates Miss M," Ava said.

Emily reeled from the pronouncement of enmity, as well as from the offhand way she said it, as if it was common, accepted knowledge. She hadn't known Larry hated her. She'd thought he just hated everyone.

As the girls went through their stretches, Emily asked Thomas with a low voice, "Any idea why Larry hates me?"

Thomas looked at her and she saw nothing but tenderness in his eyes. "Don't feel bad, Miss M. First of all, Larry is crazy. Second, he hates you because you aren't from here."

"So you think he'll soften toward me as the years move on?"

Thomas shook his head slowly. "You can teach here forever but you still won't be born here. But really, don't worry about it. He's the *janitor*, and plenty of other people have your back."

Practice was a lot more fun this time: they had catcher's equipment.

Juniper helped MacKenzie get strapped in, which was a process as everything was too big for her.

"You probably should've gotten a size small," Thomas said.

"I did," Emily said.

When she was finally in, MacKenzie ran around in a circle, giggling. "How am I supposed to move in this stuff?"

"Catch the ball, and you won't have to move much," Juniper said.

WINDMILLS

Everyone took turns throwing to MacKenzie. If the ball came anywhere near her, she stopped it. When the ball didn't come near her, Thomas chased it down. When Emily worried about MacKenzie's legs tiring, she started having her throw down to an imaginary second base, and had the other girls take turns catching her throws. That was frightful. At first, MacKenzie's throws weren't even close to true, but slowly she homed in. But even when the ball went straight into the waiting glove, most of the girls couldn't catch it. Juniper could, of course, but Emily didn't think Juniper would be playing much shortstop. Hailey could. So could Ava. And Jasmine could, but everything Jasmine did seemed to be in slow motion. Emily wondered, not for the first time, how she was going to field a softball team with only five players.

Jake Jasper showed up early again, and caught the tail end of the throw-down drill. Emily found herself embarrassed that he was seeing it. She didn't want him to think she was a bad coach. She called the girls in a few minutes early.

"Great job, guys. This has been quite a week, and given the circumstances, you look really, *really* good. Next week, we'll start hitting, and maybe we can even get outside."

"It's *freezing* out," Sydney whined.

Emily ignored her.

"So cool," Juniper said. "In Mattawooptock, we wouldn't be outside for another three weeks."

Emily tried to hide her surprise at such an almost-positive statement delivered by Juniper's lips.

"Why?" Sydney asked her.

"There's still like three feet of snow there," Juniper said, her tone returning to baseline snark.

"Is Matta-whatever really that far north?" Sydney said.

"No," Juniper said, her annoyance thick, "but you do realize that there's less snow on the coast, right? Geesh, do you ever get off this island?"

Sydney looked properly put in her place and muttered something Emily was glad she couldn't hear.

"So, Monday we'll plan to practice inside, and I'll let you know then what we'll do with the rest of the week. Those of you who don't have gloves, please try to get them this weekend."

They huddled up, yelled "Panthers!" and then dispersed.

DeAnna approached. "You said *you* were going to get me a glove."

"And I will, DeAnna."

"But you just told us all to get our own."

Emily tried to keep the annoyance out of her voice. "Did you want me to single you out? I'll get you a glove, DeAnna, but I was going to keep that between you and me."

"Oh." And with nothing else to say on the matter, DeAnna turned and walked out of the gym.

Everyone else had already left, which made it odd that Jake was still standing by the doorway. As she stood staring at him, he approached. He took long, athletic strides, and there was a bounce in his step. His lips were smiling, as were his dark brown eyes. "Lookin' good, Coach," he said, and she didn't know if he meant the team or her. She thought probably the team.

"Thanks," she said, several seconds after social norms dictated she should have.

He came to a stop in front of her and scooped a lock of hair off his forehead. "I was wondering, and please feel free to say no if this is inappropriate, but I was wondering if you would like to get a drink with me this weekend."

Her jaw fell open. Then she snapped it shut. Then it fell open again—a little. She frantically searched her brain for words. Ones that would make sense.

He laughed, breaking the silence. "Like I said, you can say no. No hard feelings."

"Thank you," she managed, "but I'm … I'm …" *embarrassed? socially crippled? wishing I were dead right now?* "I'm engaged," she managed. Then, "sort of."

He held his hands up. "I apologize, I didn't know. Though I should have figured that someone would've scooped you up." He smiled. "Sort of."

She tittered, simultaneously wishing he would go away and stay and say more nice things.

"OK, I'll leave you to it then. But, seriously, good job with the team. Juniper really likes you."

She thought this last part was a lie, but she said, "Thank you." And then she watched him walk out of the gym.

And then, as she picked up the last few stray balls, as she locked up the athletic locker, as she drove home, as she fed the cats and watered her plants, she argued with herself over whether or not to tell James. He wouldn't like it. She didn't want to upset him. She also didn't want him to think that she was trying to make him jealous. Which she wasn't.

Right? And if not, then why tell him? Because she had to. Or it was lying. Lying by omission or something. So she should tell him. But he wouldn't like it. And then around the loop again her busy brain would go.

"What are you not telling me?" James asked.

They were at The Big Dipper, waiting for their meals. She took a deep breath, then let it all out in one exhale: "Jake Jasper asked me out, but I didn't want to tell you because I don't want you to be mad, but I had to tell you or you would think I was hiding it and be mad anyway."

For several seconds, his expression was impassive, but then his face softened into a grin, and he reached for her hand. "Thank you for telling me. I'm not angry. Unless of course, you said yes?"

She thought he was kidding. "Of course not."

"Well, then, I can't say I'm surprised. You're a beautiful, amazing woman. He's a single guy. Why wouldn't he ask you out?" He leaned back. "But speaking of surprises, I am putting the boat in on Tuesday."

"Already?"

"Sure. Why not. With the weather we've been having? Season will be in full swing before we know it." He paused. "And I was wondering if you wanted to go out with me on Saturday?"

Her eyes widened. "Sure!"

"Yeah?" He looked a little surprised.

"Yeah, of course. Why wouldn't I want to get up before sunrise and go out on the freezing cold ocean?"

He gave her a dazzling smile, and she felt herself melt into it. "That's my girl. You can be my sternman."

Chapter 23

Ava had been right. Larry had set the pitching machine up for baseball. Victoria let Emily know during first period, so she snuck into the empty gym during her prep period for a peek. She looked the machine over closely, but couldn't see any way to make it fit a softball. And there certainly weren't any extra attachments lying around. She became angry with herself for not being able to figure it out, and she was even angrier that she wouldn't dare ask Larry for help.

After several minutes of staring at the ancient machine, she gave up and went back to her room. She looked at the piles of papers that needed grading, and then opted instead to flip open her laptop and check the weather report. Tuesday: 31 degrees and snow flurries. Probably shouldn't be practicing outside on that day. But Wednesday was supposed to be 50 degrees. And Thursday and Friday, 55 and 58.

During lunch, Hannah unwittingly prophesied to Emily. "My dad took me to the batting cages in Rockland yesterday!" she said, her voice high-pitched with excitement. "And I actually hit the ball!"

Seconds after the final bell rang, Emily had beaten half the kids out of the building and was on her way to James's house. She didn't even wait for him to invite her in, which she knew he was reluctant to do. She just brushed past him. He left the door standing open three inches, just in case anyone was watching and might think the two of them were about to sin.

"What time will you get back from fishing tomorrow?"

He scrunched his brows. "Why?"

"I was wondering if you wanted to help me take my entire team to the batting cages in Rockland?" She tried to make this sound fun, as she knew it wouldn't be much fun for him.

After several seconds of processing, he asked, reasonably, "Don't you have a batting cage in the gym?"

She was prepared for this argument. "Yes, but this will be way better. Outside, fresh air, several girls batting at the same time, and then we can all get ice cream!"

"Are you sure they're even open? And it's going to be cold tomorrow, you know."

"Yes, they're open." *Thank you, Hannah.* "And yes, it will be cold, but they won't be outside for very long."

"And you have a budget for this? Or is Travis Payne footing the bill?"

"No, I'll pay for it. How much can it be?"

"At least five dollars per kid for balls and then at least five dollars per kid for ice cream. Plus the ferry fares."

Yikes. She hadn't really thought about that part of it. "You don't think it's a good idea."

"I do think it's a good idea, but I don't think you should go tomorrow. Most of these girls have never hit a ball before, right? And I'm assuming they don't all have batting gloves, as we didn't buy any yesterday"—(James and she had gone to the mainland the day before to buy DeAnna's gear)—"so batting in that cold is going to cause a wicked sting, and then they'll all be afraid to bat for the rest of the year."

Drats. She hadn't thought of that.

"So, I think it's a good idea, but I think you should do it on Friday."

"Yeah?" She didn't try to hide her surprise. "And you'll go with us?"

"Of course. You might also want to invite a parent or two along. Though Jasper wouldn't be my first choice."

She looked up at him quickly, but his eyes were twinkling.

"So why don't you tell me what this is really about?" he asked. "Can't get the batting machine to spit softballs?"

She didn't know if he was a brilliant detective, he just could read her that well, or both. Whatever it was, she loved him for it.

"Yeah. Something like that."

He looked at his wrist. "We've got time. Let's go take a look at it."

"Really?" She wanted to kiss him. Over and over again.

"Well, I'm not promising I can fix it. But I'll try."

Within ten minutes, James had found the softball attachment and two buckets of batting machine softballs deep in the bowels of a storage closet Emily hadn't known existed. They patiently waited for the baseball team to finish practice, and then, after another twenty minutes, James had the rickety machine firing softballs. The girls huddled around the cage, most of them champing at the bit. Emily told them over and over to get their fingers out of the net.

WINDMILLS

While James tried to get the relic to fire strikes, Emily forced the girls to endure a basic batting stance lecture. They all acted as though they understood and would do as she instructed—she knew that for most of them, neither of these things were true.

Juniper went in first. And of course, she hit every strike. It was difficult to tell how hard she was hitting it, but at least she was hitting it. While she was on her second bucket of balls, Hailey came alongside Emily.

"Miss M? Some of us are worried about the batting helmets."

Oh no. Not again. "What about them?"

"Well, not to be mean, but DeAnna has had lice, and so no one wants to share with her."

"*Has* had lice? As in she doesn't have lice now?"

Hailey gave her a "be reasonable" look. "Come on, Miss M. You've *got* to understand this. We're not trying to be mean, but DeAnna doesn't even shower. Her hair is super greasy even if she doesn't have lice. Can't she just have a designated helmet?"

At first, Emily didn't know what to do. Then she decided not to do anything. "I'm not going to do that to her. You and the other girls who are worried might want to go buy your own helmet."

Hailey stood there for a few seconds, then appeared to give up, and walked away.

Ava's form was terrible, but she made contact with nearly every pitch. And to her credit, she did at least try to implement Emily's corrections.

And Hannah—sweet Hannah—Hannah was a thing of beauty with a bat. Over and over—crack! Over and over James would duck or dodge the line drive trying to injure him as he fed the machine. "Nice work, Hannah!" Emily praised. "I had no idea you had that in you!"

"I told you I like to hit things," Hannah said, giving Emily a broad smile as she took off her helmet. Then she rubbed her belly. "Finally those extra Doritos and Funny Bones are going to come in handy."

Emily smiled. "I don't think that's it. And none of that stuff during softball season."

"I didn't see that specified in my contract," Hannah said and sauntered off.

She looked at Thomas. "Shoot! I forgot all about contracts! I was supposed to have them sign one, wasn't I?"

"You were supposed to," Thomas said. "But don't worry, this is the first official practice, right? So you're not even late yet."

"Maybe not, but I will be! I don't even know where to get such a thing," she whispered out of the side of her mouth while looking into the cage. It was Sydney's turn, and she couldn't hit the broad side of a barn.

"Want me to go find one and make copies?"

She looked at him. "Seriously?"

He shrugged. "Sure, why not? I'm not super busy right now."

"How are you going to find a copy?"

"I have my ways."

"Thomas, what would I do without you?"

"You'd have to go teach at a real high school. I'll be right back," and he was off.

The girls acted as though it was perfectly normal that Thomas was the one handing out the contracts, and then signed them without so much as glancing at the content. Emily wondered if she should have gone over the contract with them, but it was already 5:30 and she figured the basketball players, at least, had probably read it before. Besides, how many of these girls were drinkers or smokers?

Chapter 24

By Wednesday when they all arrived at the field on Cobblestone Street, everyone had a glove and a pair of cleats. A few girls had their own batting helmet; Sydney's was bright pink, which Emily thought might not work well with the red stripes in their uniforms, and wished she'd been more specific when she told them to get their own helmets. *Oh well. Too late now*.

It was time to try some fielding. She lined half the girls up at first, and half at third. Then she picked up a bat and headed toward home plate. "Juniper, would you please demonstrate the stance they should take to be ready for the ball?"

Juniper acted pained, but she demonstrated. Emily hit her the ball, and she flawlessly scooped it up and fired it to first base, where it bounced off the outside of Hannah's glove. *I wish I could play Juniper everywhere.*

Hailey stood behind Juniper. "OK, Hailey, you're up. Hannah, why don't you try to catch another one?"

Emily hit the ball. Hailey bobbled it, but she did stop it, got it into her hand, and then fired it three feet over Hannah's head.

"Let's try that again," Emily said. And they did. And again. And again.

After thirty minutes, when Sydney complained about being cold, and Emily told them to run a couple of laps, Emily had determined that only Juniper and Ava could field the ball. MacKenzie and Hailey were close. But since Juniper and MacKenzie were likely to be otherwise engaged, that meant that Ava and Hailey had to play the entire infield. Well, that wasn't entirely true; Jasmine could catch the ball fairly well, but she sure couldn't throw it—she was shaping up to be a fine first baseman.

The girls returned from their laps; Sara Crockett, dressed all in black, led the pack. Sara had even found a black softball glove and a black batting helmet. Her cleats were mostly black too, but the constancy was interrupted by a pink logo that Emily thought probably drove Sara nuts.

Sara was a pleasant surprise. She was doing much better outside than she had in the gym. She was still fairly terrible, but Emily had to give her an A for effort. She seemed one hundred percent focused, both mentally and physically, and when she dove for a grounder, Emily wanted to give her a trophy on the spot.

Emily sent them into the outfield and then tried to hit them some balls. The first one didn't quite get there. The second one she whiffed entirely, and was grateful that she didn't hear any scoffing or giggles. *This is harder than it looks.* She picked up another ball, threw it up into the air, swung with all her might, made contact, and beamed with pride as she watched it soar through the air and then fall to the ground thirty feet in front of the outfielders—she hadn't even made it out of the infield.

Juniper came running toward her. "Want me to take over?"

Emily *didn't* want her to take over, didn't want to admit that she couldn't do this, and didn't want to give this uncoachable kid any proof that her coach wasn't really much of a coach. "Sure. Thanks," she said, not liking the overwhelming feeling of humility that was making her feel sick to her stomach.

WINDMILLS

But Juniper didn't give her any attitude. She just hit the ball. Right to Chloe. Who didn't catch it. Then she hit another ball. To Lucy. Who also didn't catch it.

Emily trotted out to the outfield to try to provide some help. "OK, guys. When the ball is hit to you, you've got to try to judge where it's going. Is it going over your head? Or is it going to land in front of you? That determines which direction you're going to want to move, and you'll get better at that the more balls you see come your way. Now you don't want to run with your glove in the air. You just run, like normal. And then try to get under the ball. Then get your glove up, and your throwing hand right beside your glove. Understand?" Sixteen blank stares. "OK, let's try it again. Sydney, you're up."

Juniper hit the ball right to her. Sydney ran forward, holding her glove up in the air like a torch to light a dark path, about thirty feet, then turned and watched the ball soar over her head.

"Next," Emily said.

Juniper hit the ball to Sara, who took two quick steps forward, then turned and ran four steps back, and then caught the ball.

Emily couldn't help it. She yelped with excitement, jumped up and down and clapped like a little kid on a Ferris wheel. "Sara! Yes! Yes! Yes!"

Sara remained expressionless, but Emily sensed she was enjoying herself. Or at least she was less angry than usual. The combination of cold and exercise was also causing some pink to break through the pale foundation caked on her cheeks.

Through the line they went, over and over—and over and over, no one came anywhere near catching it—except Sara.

After a few rounds, Emily jogged back to Juniper. When it was Sara's turn, Emily said to Juniper, "Hit it over her this time."

Juniper raised an eyebrow. "Feeling cruel?"

"No, not at all. Just want to see something."

Juniper hit the ball and Sara didn't even hesitate. She seemed to know as soon as it left the bat that it was going deep, and she turned and ran for it. She almost got under it, didn't quite, and then dove for it with her glove outstretched.

"Unreal," Emily said.

"Yeah, that was pretty good," Juniper admitted.

"I think I've just found my new favorite human being."

Chapter 25

On Friday, the big news was that Bojack had been sprung. There was quite a debate raging as to whether he'd figure he was in enough trouble or would be eager to make more. Would he lie low or come back raging? The jury was divided.

At lunchtime, the social studies teacher asked Emily which way she was betting.

"I have no idea, Kyle. I don't know Bojack. I would *hope* he would keep his nose clean, for everyone's sake, but of course I have no idea what he'll do."

"He's not going to keep his nose clean. He's been in and out of jail for years."

"For what?"

"Mostly domestic violence, I think."

Emily's stomach lurched. "What do you mean? Whom did he hurt?"

Kyle shrugged. "I can't remember when his last arrest was. I don't exactly keep track. But I'm pretty sure he's abused every woman he's ever dated, and I doubt DeAnna's mother would be any different."

"What about DeAnna?"

"What about her?"

"Does he hurt her?"

"Emily, how should I know?"

Emily began to walk away, but Kyle grabbed her arm. "Don't do it."

She pulled her arm away. "Do what?"

"For once, will you just stay out of other people's business? It's not our job to get involved in this stuff."

"Sure," she said. Then she walked over to DeAnna's table. Only then did she notice that Juniper had moved over to the table Blake usually sat at—the cool table. Juniper was sandwiched between Blake and Thomas. Chloe was perched on the other side of Thomas, though there was barely enough room. She looked miserable, as though she might fall off the end of the bench any second.

"Hi, DeAnna," Emily said, sliding onto the bench across from her.

"What." Her tone was flat and unencouraging.

"So I hear Bojack is coming home?"

"So."

"So, is that a good thing?"

DeAnna looked at her, her eyes vapid. "I don't know what you're talking about."

"I heard he was getting out of jail. Is that true?"

She shrugged and looked down at her American chop suey. "My mom bailed him out."

"DeAnna, can I ask you an awkward question?"

DeAnna cocked her head to the side. "What?"

"Are you OK at home? Are you safe?"

"What?"

"I'm asking if you are safe in your own home. If you are in danger, from Bojack or anything else, we can help you."

DeAnna slammed her fork down on her tray, splattering spaghetti sauce onto the table, then stood up and hissed, "Of course I'm safe. I can take care of myself! Just stay out of my life!"And as soon as she had untangled her legs from the bench seat, DeAnna stomped toward the tray return. Emily stood too, though more slowly and less dramatically, and taking great care not to make eye contact with Kyle. She didn't want to give him the satisfaction.

Given this prelude, Emily wasn't shocked when DeAnna didn't turn up at the ferry for their big trip to the batting cages. Emily was a little surprised to see that everyone else did—including Thomas, who handed her a check from his dad.

"Dad said you shouldn't have to coach for free *and* pay for all this, so he wanted to help." This time, she felt a little uneasy taking the money, but she still took it. She didn't know what else to do. Emily had asked Chloe's and MacKenzie's mothers along for the trip, so they had four adults, sixteen teenage girls, and Thomas—one big happy family.

In the batting cages the emotional, hormonal teens turned into joyous little kids who just wanted more quarters. It was a bit too chaotic for Emily to get any real coaching in, but she managed to wedge in the occasional "Put your weight on your back foot" and "Loosen your grip on the bat." She also heard James putting in his two cents. The two mom chaperones, sisters Gina and Heather, sat on a picnic table and talked, ignoring the entire scene, which Emily thought was entirely reasonable.

When Emily ran out of quarters, the girls all scooted over to the ice cream stand, some a little faster than others. MacKenzie and Lucy literally ran. Her team's orders made Emily realize just how young these girls were: bubble gum ice cream in sugar cones; Superman with sprinkles; and lots of cotton candy soft serve.

Gina and Heather tried to pay for their kids' treats, but Emily, without thinking, said, "Don't worry, I'm not paying for it. Travis gave us money for this."

The cheery smile fled Gina's face. Heather's smile stayed, but it looked strained.

Gina pushed the bills in her hand at Emily. "In that case, I insist. Our family doesn't take charity from Travis Payne." She spat the word "Payne."

"I don't think it's charity," Emily tried. "He's just supportive of ..." Gina had already walked away, so Emily stopped talking.

Heather was still holding money out toward her. "She's not upset with you, Emily. Her husband is *very* opposed to this whole windmill thing. Don't take it personally."

Emily took the outstretched money, and looked at MacKenzie's mom. "But you are for the windmills, aren't you? So you guys aren't on the same side in this?"

"Ah, we've disagreed on everything our whole lives." She laughed. "This will all be over soon and we'll still be sisters. And just because I think the windmills are a good idea doesn't mean I'm a big Travis Payne fan. He can be incredibly manipulative."

"I don't think Travis supporting the softball team has anything to do with the windmills."

Heather looked thoughtful for a few seconds and then said, "I'm afraid it has *everything* to do with the windmills." And then she rejoined her sister, leaving Emily standing and feeling quite alone.

Emily looked around at her charge and tried not to think about what had just transpired. She noticed Hannah wasn't eating. "Don't you want anything, hon?"

Hannah shook her head. "No, thank you, not hungry."

Emily thought this probably wasn't the case, but wasn't sure how to encourage her to join in, or if she even *should* encourage her to partake in something unhealthy. So instead she decided to join Hannah in her fast. She didn't really need the sugar either.

James, apparently feeling no such conviction, enthusiastically ordered a triple scoop of maple walnut. As Emily looked around at all the youthful neon-colored desserts, she thought sure maple walnut was an old man choice. This thought made her heart warm.

WINDMILLS

The girls begged to go to Walmart afterward, but Emily refused. Though they didn't let up with their petitions until they were actually on the ferry, Emily stood firm. "What's so exciting about Walmart?" she muttered to James as the mainland shrunk behind them.

"To these kids, Walmart is the mall. Some of them don't get off the island much."

Chapter 26

The first of April dawned crisp and clear. Emily's alarm went off at five, giving her plenty of time for a shower, but she decided she was too cold and tired for a shower, so opted for a pot of coffee instead. By the time James pulled into her short driveway, she was properly caffeinated, had put on a fresh coat of makeup and pulled her hair back from her face, and was wearing almost every item of clothing she owned.

When James saw her, he laughed. "It's not going to be *that* cold out there."

She was annoyed. "If I hadn't worn enough clothes, you'd be making fun of *that*."

James's expression grew serious, and made her feel guilty. "I'm not making fun of you, Emily. It was just cute."

She raised an eyebrow. "Cute?"

He opened the truck door for her. "Yes, cute. You are the cutest sternman I've ever had."

"Thank you." She still felt a bit cranky but tried not to. She *was* grateful James was doing this for her; she just wasn't much of a morning person. "I'm not complaining, but why do you have to start this early?"

James took a swig from a well-worn travel mug. "Actually, I'm usually already on the water by now. But to answer your question, we get an early start because they say that's when the bugs are most active. To answer your other question, *we're* getting an early start because I wanted to show you the sunrise."

That squashed whatever crankiness remained. "Thank you, James. That's sweet. I've never seen the sun rise over the ocean."

"Most people haven't." He pointed to the floor by her feet. "You might want to put those on."

She looked down to see a giant pair of muck boots.

"I know they'll be too big," he said, apparently reading her mind, "but my deck can get sloppy, even if we're not fishing, and I don't want your feet to get cold."

She slid her double-stockinged feet into the spacious rubber boots. "*Can* we fish?"

He grinned broadly. "We can if you want. I'm not going to fish all day with you—you'd likely hate me, but we can pull up a string if you want to see what it's like, or we can just go for a boat ride. Either way is fine with me. Whatever you want."

My, you're being awfully gallant. What are you up to?

James parked the truck and quickly came around to her side. She didn't need any help to climb out of the truck, but he gave her a hand anyway, then held her hand all the way to the dock; he let go of her briefly as he jumped into the skiff, but then he grabbed her hand again to help her in, treating her like a fragile china doll.

She sat down on the cold wooden seat and tucked her gloved hands between her knees. James threw off the lines and then gracefully sat down and took up the oars. Dawn was breaking, and the sky had turned a gorgeous shade of grayish blue, making Emily feel as if she were sitting under a firmament of blue quartz.

As James began to row, Emily couldn't help but admire him. She couldn't see his muscles moving under his bulky Carhartt, but she knew they were there. The water was mostly calm except for a small swell, but their movement through the water blew the wisps that had escaped her ponytail back off her face. She suddenly felt inexplicably elated and took a deep breath of the sweet, salty air. The taste of it on her tongue only brought her more joy, and though she knew she was grinning like a fool, she couldn't help it.

It soon became obvious which boat he was rowing toward, a clean white boat with "Piercehaven, Maine" stretched across the stern. Above that, large red letters spelled out "Sally." Absurdly, a pang of jealousy stabbed Emily's chest. "Who's Sally?"

"My grandmother."

"Oh." Remorse prevented her from saying more.

But James didn't seem to notice her question's green tint. He just continued, "My father's mother. Her husband, my grandfather, is the one who taught me to fish."

"How old were you?"

"When I really started? I was thirteen when I started going out with him in the summer, but he took me out for fun long before that. I don't even remember my first trips, I was so young. He was a good grandpa. A good man. A good fisherman."

They reached the mooring, James tied off, and then helped Emily aboard Sally. The first thing she noticed was the smell. She was afraid she might actually gag, and that, she was sure, *would* offend the man of her dreams. "Do you have actual bait on here, or is that just a lingering after-smell?"

He laughed. "Sorry, I don't even notice it. Yes, it's actual bait. And it's a day old, so it's extra stinky, which, by the way, makes it extra effective." James started the boat with a key that was already in the ignition.

"That's gross."

"Yes, it is. But if you think about it, bugs are pretty gross too."

Emily knew that by "bugs," James meant lobsters. She didn't know why islanders called them bugs, and she didn't ask. "Yes, but people think they're delicious," she said. "And will pay a pretty penny for them."

"I wish they'd pay more."

"So you're not afraid of people stealing your boat?"

"What?"

"I noticed you left the keys in the ignition."

"Oh, no, people have been shot for less."

She didn't say anything.

"I mean, *I* wouldn't shoot anyone, but people don't know that—for sure—and besides, who would want to steal Sally? They'd never get away with it. She's one of a kind—they'd have to do so much work to her to change her, it would be easier just to buy a boat of their own.

Now, people have occasionally stolen the *lobsters*, though they always get caught—"

"How?"

"This is a tight knit community. We have eyes and ears everywhere." He winked at her. "And security cameras. And people have stolen boats in order to *sink* them, but never just to take them."

"What?"

"Oh yeah, people get in territory disputes and they do crazy things. Fishing can get violent."

Emily looked skeptical.

"Not today though," James said with bravado. "I'll protect you." He turned on his radar and radio. Then he turned and grabbed a gaff, which he used to pull the mooring buoy closer so that he could unhook it. Then he gave her another big smile. "You ready?"

She nodded, her heart bursting with admiration. James seemed so proud to be sharing this part of his life with her, and she couldn't believe how full her heart felt in that moment. She almost couldn't smell the bait anymore. He pushed the throttle forward and they were off. She reached for a bulkhead to steady herself, and noticed two pair of oil pants hanging on hooks. "Do we have to wear those?"

He grinned again, or maybe he hadn't stopped grinning. "Only if you're going to help me pull traps. Or fill bait bags."

"I think I should."

He raised a luscious eyebrow. "Oh yeah?"

"Yeah." In that moment, Emily couldn't believe how much she wanted to help him pull up a lobster trap.

Chapter 27

"What color are your buoys?" Emily asked.

They were puttering along at a pretty good clip now, and Emily wanted to know what colors to be on the lookout for.

"Orange and black. My grandfather picked 'em, so don't blame me for the Halloween theme. And we're nowhere near them yet. I thought I'd take you for a little spin.

"Oh yeah? Where?"

"To the east side of the island." He pointed out the sights as they went. His dad's boat, his buddy's boat, Thomas's house, the school, the small public beach. Then he pulled into a little cove and cut the engine.

"What are you doing?" Emily asked, alarmed. "Won't we drift ashore?"

He chuckled. "No. We'll be fine. The tide's going out, and we won't be here long."

"Where's here?"

"Here is the east side of the island. More specifically, this is called "P-I-G—and don't say that word out loud—Poop Cove.""

"Don't say what out loud?"

"P-I-G," he spelled again.

"What?"

"We call it Bacon Poop Cove, because that way we can avoid the p-word and also because it's funny to say bacon poop."

"Why can't you say the p-word?"

"It's bad luck. So that"—he pointed toward a point of land jutting out into the water—"is Bacon Poop Point. That's where my grandfather shot his first partridge. And this is Bacon Poop Cove."

"You don't seriously believe in bad luck?"

"Of course not." He sat down on a bench that ran alongside part of the port gunwale and then pulled her onto his lap and wrapped his arms around her. He *had* put on the oil pants, and the plastic felt freezing cold through her blue jeans. She shivered, though she wasn't sure it was entirely from the cold—his thick, long arms wrapped around her waist might have had something to do with it.

"Then why won't you say the p-word?"

"I don't think my DNA will allow it," he whispered into her ear, causing every inch of her body to break out in goosebumps. "Look," he said. She looked.

The infinite shades of pink that had owned the horizon only seconds ago had been interrupted by a burst of brilliant yellow. A sliver of sun had broken over the horizon and the raw beauty of it stole Emily's breath. One can photograph a sunrise. One can paint it. One can describe it in a poem. But no one can truly capture it. There's nothing like seeing it live and in person.

"We are now two of the very first people in the whole country to see the sun come up," James said in a voice so soft she could hardly believe it was his.

"Aren't we going to go blind looking at this?"

"If we were, I'd have been blind long ago. Besides, we're not going to stare at it for long." He slowly loosed his arms from around her and slid out from behind her, leaving her sitting on the cool wooden bench. Then he knelt in front of her.

Immediately she knew what was happening and immediately her head filled with absurd thoughts: *Is he just doing this because Jake asked me out? Is this an April fools joke?* She took a deep breath and forced herself to get out of her own head.

"You OK?" He smiled. "You look a little pale." He reached into his pocket and pulled out a small black velvety box. And then he flipped it open to reveal a dainty golden band with a brilliant sparkling diamond. "As promised, here is your official marriage proposal. I know we haven't known each other very long, but I have no doubts that you are the woman God wants me to marry. We can have a nice long engagement if you want, but I just wanted to make sure you knew how serious I am about us." He took a breath. "So, let's make it official. Emily Morse, will you marry me?"

"Of course!" The words flew out of her as if they'd been held back by a rubber band. She flung her arms around his neck. "Of course," she said again, softly, her eyes staring at the horizon as it filled with a gold so bright it could only have been supernatural.

James had left his mooring with no intention of pulling traps that day, but Emily talked him into it, although she didn't do any of the physical pulling—he wouldn't let her. He did offer to let her put new bait in the traps, but she couldn't make herself do it. As the sun ascended, a quick breeze began to blow, which blew most of the smell away, but she still didn't want to touch the small, slimy dead fish, even though James offered her gloves.

She was far more content to watch him work and after only about four traps did she realize that the work was indeed repetitive. Still, it was more hypnotically rhythmic than redundant, and when he'd finished pulling up one string, she talked him into another. But then he called it quits. "I'm heading in. I'm spending more than I'm making right now." She was disappointed, but she was also frozen. And it was true that they hadn't caught much. He'd put four lobsters in the live tank and thrown far more than that back into the water. She'd been amazed at how quickly he could tell their size.

"Don't you have to measure them?"

"Sometimes. Not usually," he'd said and flung a small one over his shoulder, its legs flailing on its way home. "I know a keeper when I see it," he'd said with a wink.

Now she said, "Not very many other boats out here, huh?"

"Not yet. There will be."

"Why do you start so early in the season?"

"I don't know. Just always have. Like to get a head start. Mark my territory and all that. Plus the price is good right now. It'll drop when we all get out on the water." He looked at her and gave her a broad smile. "Any other questions?"

"Just one. Do our wedding colors have to be black and orange?"

Chapter 28

Emily woke up the following Saturday feeling anxious. It took her a second to remember why. *Oh yeah, we have a scrimmage today.* She was so excited to see these girls in a game situation. They had come so far. Four of them could even throw the ball now. And five of them could catch it. But she was also nervous. She felt protective of her kids, and didn't want them to be embarrassed. They were so used to winning. This would be different. Very different.

But as she stood at her kitchen counter watching the coffee drip into the pot with excruciating slowness, she noticed it looked a bit wet outside. It had rained. She looked up. No blue sky in sight. She couldn't check a weather app like a normal person because she didn't have a cell signal or internet connection. But she did have the next best thing to a weather app—she had a lobsterman. Impatiently she poured a cup of coffee from the incomplete pot and took a gulp of too-strong scalding coffee. Then she dialed her fiancé from her landline.

"You sound like you've been up for hours," she said when he answered.

"I have. You sound like you just woke up."

"I did. I'm calling for a weather forecast."

"Ah, I see. Well, it doesn't look good. I'd call it off unless you want your girls' first game to be a soaking wet freezing cold experience."

"Isn't it up to Camden Christian to call it off though?"

"It is. But you live on an island. If you call them up and say, 'Hey I'd like to cancel the ferry trip ASAP, so let's cancel the game,' they would."

Emily sighed. "That stinks. I don't want to cancel."

"I know, but you also don't want them playing in the rain. They'll get hurt. And since they're probably going to get mercied, they'll also get discouraged."

"I don't think the mercy rule applies to a scrimmage, James. And I also don't think we're going to get *mercied* by Camden Christian. What have they got, thirty kids in the whole school? And don't count my girls out. They've been looking a lot better lately."

"OK, OK, don't get defensive. But you called for a weather forecast, and I'm telling you that it's going to rain and the wind's going to blow. It's going to be cold."

"OK, thanks." She knew he was right. "I'll call the coach."

"Good. Then we can do something else today."

"Lunch at The Big Dipper?" she guessed. It wasn't a wild guess.

"Hey, did you hear about that?" He sounded excited.

"Hear about what?" She stretched out the phone cord as far as it would go so she could sit at her kitchen table, suddenly wishing she was sitting at James's kitchen table.

"About The Big Dipper. Travis tried to take his family to eat there, and they refused to serve him."

"You're kidding."

"I am not. They all came in, sat down, waited for a while, and were completely ignored. Finally, Abby went and asked one of the servers to take their order, and the server said she was told not to serve them. So they left."

Emily felt sick. "Was Thomas there?"

"I believe so."

"That's awful. I don't care if you disagree with someone, you don't treat people like that."

"Well, people are feeling desperate. They really don't want this to happen."

"Oh, for crying out loud. It's two windmills. They're not putting in a nuclear facility. It's not that big a deal—"

"It *is* that big a deal," James interrupted, "if you've lived on Chicken Hill your whole life, if you're living on the land your grandparents were raised on, and suddenly someone wants to put up a giant, loud eyesore in your backyard."

"James, it's not going to be *that* loud."

"Tell that to the people on Vinalhaven. Anyway, these people shouldn't have to stare at windmills for the rest of their lives if they don't want to."

"James, anywhere else, people have to deal with this stuff all the time. Cell phone towers going up. Billboards. Tall buildings. You can't control what your neighbors do."

"This isn't anywhere else, Emily." Something in his tone made her stomach lurch.

"James, are you mad at me about this?"

"No, Emily, I'm not mad. But if you're going to be an islander, you might want to start thinking like an islander."

"I'm pretty sure Travis and Abby are islanders too, James."

"No, Travis and Abby are moneygrubbers."

Chapter 29

The softball and baseball teams' first countable games were scheduled to be against Buckfield. At Buckfield. This wasn't great news. Emily kicked herself for not scheduling more than one preseason scrimmage, but the time had just flown by so fast. Now here they were, only days away from real games against real teams. She didn't know anything about the Buckfield softball team except that they'd had pretty incredible records for the last several years. So she assumed they had a girl who could pitch.

So far, she hadn't let Juniper pitch batting practice. She hadn't wanted to wear her out or risk her getting hurt, but now she was out of time. Her girls should probably face a human pitcher before facing the Buckfield one. And she didn't know any windmiller she could ask to spend three hours on a ferry just to pitch batting practice.

So, on Monday, she had MacKenzie get into full catcher's gear and she put Juniper on the mound. "Hailey, you're up. Chloe, you're on deck."

The first pitch went by Hailey so fast she didn't even begin her swing. She looked at Emily. "Don't worry, I'm OK, just taking a look at it."

The second pitch went by Hailey—and then she swung. She looked at Emily again. "I'm still OK."

The third pitch went by Hailey at the same time as she swung, but she made no contact.

"Don't take your eye off the ball, Hailey," Emily said.

Hailey didn't respond. She just looked mad. She swung again. And again. And again. And no contact. Emily knew she had to move on to Chloe, but she didn't want to pull Hailey out of the batter's box before she even got a piece of the ball. Turns out, she didn't have to make the decision. Hailey made it. She swore, ripped off her batting helmet, and threw it at the bench. Then she dramatically tore her batting gloves off too.

Emily nodded to Chloe, who sheepishly took Hailey's spot at the plate. Emily went over to Hailey. "And now you can have a seat."

"What?" Hailey snapped.

"I said, have a seat," Emily said, her voice rising. She knew half the field heard her, but she didn't care. "First of all, Juniper is an awesome pitcher. Of *course* you're not going to be able to hit off her the first time you try. So don't get so discouraged. Second of all, you don't get to act like that. You're a leader here. So have a seat until you can act like it." Emily turned to walk away.

"Coach," Hailey said.

Emily turned back toward her.

"I'm sorry. I'll act like it. Can I go back out on the field, please?"

Emily nodded and then turned her attention to Chloe, who wasn't faring much better than Hailey had. "You're just throwing it down the middle, right?" Emily asked Juniper.

"Yes, ma'am."

"Nothing fancy? No curveballs or drop balls?"

Juniper gave her an odd look.

"What?"

Juniper jogged off the mound and up to Emily. Then she lifted her glove to her mouth and spoke through it. "I don't want anyone to know this, but I can't throw a curveball or drop ball."

Emily laughed.

Juniper looked annoyed.

Emily put a hand on her shoulder. "Don't be offended, hon. I'm not laughing at you, I swear. It just struck me funny the way you delivered the news."

Juniper nodded, looking serious, then lifted her glove to her lips again. "I can throw a change-up," she muttered.

Emily nodded and gently pushed her back toward the mound. "OK, well don't throw any right now."

Chloe didn't make contact and looked considerably less coordinated than Hailey had while trying. Jasmine was next.

"I like that strike zone," Juniper said. She was referencing Jasmine's height, but Jasmine didn't seem to know this. Jasmine couldn't hit the ball either. Neither could Allie. By the time Sydney missed ten pitches in a row, Emily could tell morale was low. The field was silent and no one was smiling. To make matters worse, some parents had gathered to watch the end of practice. This happened often, but they weren't usually subjected to such a hopeless show.

"Hey, bring it in for a second, guys," Emily called out. The girls trotted in. "OK, listen to me. Juniper here is good. It is very hard to hit off a good pitcher, especially when you're just starting to learn to bat—"

"Buckfield's pitcher is pretty good too," Sydney interrupted.

"I know that, Syd, and please don't interrupt me." Emily took a deep breath. She took a step back so she could see all their faces. "Listen, we might not get a single hit on Friday. But what I'm trying to tell you is, that's OK. This is our first game, against a great team who's going to have a great pitcher. But it's OK if we lose. It's OK if she pitches a no-hitter. Good for her. We'll still get to play defense. And we still might even get on base. Fast pitchers are also often wild pitchers, and we might get some walks." Juniper looked skeptical, but Emily ignored that. "Or maybe we'll get lucky and someone will get hit by a pitch."

"That's actually my plan," MacKenzie said, and everyone laughed.

The spell was broken. *Thank you, MacKenzie.*

"OK, so let's go back out there. And it doesn't matter if we hit or don't hit. It doesn't matter if we score or don't score. Let's go."

They all ran away from her, except Hailey, who stood there looking at her. "If none of that matters, then what is even the point?"

She took a step closer to her junior. "The point is learning a game that can be a life skill.

The point is being with your friends and teammates. The point is exercising and breathing fresh air. Winning is fun, Hailey, I know that, but losing can be fun too. Just relax and try to enjoy the game."

"I'll never be able to enjoy losing," Hailey said. But she did run back out onto the field.

Next up was Hannah, who was the first girl to swing at the first pitch. She didn't hit it, but at least she swung. And her swing was textbook. "Lookin' good, Hannah!" Emily said, and meant it. Hannah swung again at the second pitch, and the top of her bat caught the bottom of the ball, making a high-pitched ping sound, and sending the ball backward into the backstop.

The girls acted as though they'd won the World Series. Victoria jumped up and down screaming what sounded like war cries. Kylie did cartwheels. Chloe put both hands in the air and repeatedly shouted hallelujah. The only girls not smiling were DeAnna and Sara, but even Sara was slapping her glove with her throwing hand. *What a bunch of lunatics*, Emily thought, but she too had a crazy grin on her face. "OK, Hannah, let's see what happens if you hit the center of the ball. Also, MacKenzie, in real life, if a foul ball like that happens, you're going to have to rip your mask off and try to catch it."

"I'll catch it," MacKenzie said, her bravado muffled by the hardware.

Juniper wound up and fired as the team waited with bated breath. Hannah swung and, crack, hit a grounder down the first base line, toward Natalie, who leapt out of the way, letting it go by her into the outfield, where it rolled to a stop in the grass. The team went berserk again. Hannah had never been so popular.

"OK, guys, we should probably start acting like defenders. So, down and ready, and if she, excuse me, *when* she hits it, *catch* the ball! Don't jump out of the way. We can practice fielding right now too." She nodded at Juniper, who threw another pitch.

Hannah missed this time and the team let out a corporate groan.

"That was too high," Hannah called out to Juniper. Emily couldn't *see* Juniper roll her eyes because of her face mask, but she knew she did.

Juniper fired another pitch, and Hannah belted it right at Hailey, who was playing shortstop. Hailey didn't catch it, but she did knock it down.

"Hannah, you are my favorite human being right now," Emily called out.

Juniper threw another pitch, and Hannah hit this one over Hailey's head, in the direction of the giant boulder. Sara turned and gave chase. The spectators started whistling and cheering.

"OK, Hannah, let's end on that one," Emily called out. "Ava, you're up. Hannah, come here please."

Hannah trotted over to her, removing her helmet along the way and revealing a giant smile. Emily raised her eyebrows at her. "Hannah, where did *that* come from? You were great in the batting cages, but Juniper is a good pitcher!"

"Look," Hannah said, and held her hands out to Emily. Her palms were covered in blisters.

Emily looked from her hands to her eyes. "What on earth?"

Hannah looked so proud. "I've been spending some time in the batting cages."

"In *Rockland*?"

"Yep. My dad's been taking me."

"Well, tell your dad thank you!"

She laughed. "I will."

"And can you also ask him to get you some batting gloves?"

She looked confused. "Why? What do they do?"

"For one thing, they prevent blisters."

She laughed. "Little late for that. But I'll ask him. I always thought they were just for sh—"

Their conversation was interrupted by another crack of the bat. Ava had just hit the ball back to Juniper. "Nice job, Ava!" Emily called. She felt a little lightheaded. She thought maybe she was in shock. Ava hit the next pitch toward first. And the next one over the first baseman's head.

But it was there the glory ended. No one else hit the ball. No one else even came close. But it was OK. Emily was encouraged. The girls were encouraged. Even the parents in their waiting vehicles looked encouraged. It was still true that they might not get a hit off Buckfield. But it was also true that they might.

Chapter 30

Emily overslept on Friday and showed up to her classroom in a ponytail and mismatched pumps, with mascara all over her left eyelid because she'd put it on in the car.

"Whoa," Chloe said. "Are you OK?"

"Yes, why?" Emily asked, even though she had a pretty good idea why Chloe was asking.

"If I didn't know better, I'd think you were hungover," Thomas said.

"No, but I haven't had any coffee yet. Will you go get me some?" She was kidding. Mostly.

"Like from the teachers' room?" Thomas asked.

"Yes, unless they erected a Dunkin' Donuts on the island while I slept."

"My, you're cranky when you wake up. And no, I don't think I'm allowed in the teachers' room."

"Fine." Emily looked at the clock. She didn't have time to go either. *Darn it.* A screaming headache was about to commandeer her head any second now.

"Did you hear about Bojack?" Thomas asked.

Emily sat down. That's when she noticed her pumps. One black. One brown. Otherwise perfectly matched. "No. Now what?"

"He threatened to *kill* Jake Jasper yesterday," Thomas said.

"Was he drunk?"

"Oh, of course. But still! You can't threaten to *kill* someone!"

"Did they arrest him?"

"By 'they' I assume you mean the sheriff? If so, no. He hasn't. But I think he'll have to. Jake filed a formal complaint with the company. So they're not just going to let it go."

"When did it happen?"

"Yesterday afternoon. At the actual job site. Stupid Bojack drives right up to the site and falls out of his truck. Starts yelling at them to get off his land or he'll start shooting."

"*Shooting*?" Suddenly this was more interesting. "He had a *gun*?"

Thomas shrugged. "They didn't see one, but that doesn't mean he didn't have one. Lots of guys keep one in their truck."

"Isn't he a felon? Then he's not allowed to have a gun?"

Thomas snorted. "He's not allowed to drive either. But he still does. Anyway, Jake went to deal with him, told him to get off the property, which of course, *isn't his land*, and Bojack pushed him in the chest and said, 'I'm coming for you first. Get off this island or you're dead.'"

Emily was skeptical. "That sounds a bit too poetic for Bojack."

Thomas shrugged. "That's what Jake told the company."

"And who told you?"

"My dad."

"And who told your dad?"

Thomas looked stumped.

"Exactly. This is all just gossip. The only people who know what really happened are the people who were there. Unless Bojack is arrested, I'm going to assume that nothing too serious happened."

Bojack was arrested.

During first period, Emily was waxing poetic about Gwendolyn Brooks's use of line breaks when someone knocked on her open classroom door. She looked up to see Thomas standing there with a large Styrofoam cup.

"Sorry to interrupt, but it was an emergency," he said.

"Did you actually leave school?" she asked, quickly crossing the room toward him.

He shrugged. "Maybe?"

She thanked him profusely, took the coffee, and said, "I owe you huge, but you shouldn't have left school. Now get to class." Then she took the travel cover off and slugged back some of the medicine.

Thomas waited for her to swallow before he muttered, "I just heard. Sheriff arrested Bojack." Then he vanished down the hall.

"*What* a brownnoser," Tyler said, and everyone laughed.

"That'll be enough out of you, Tyler." She took another swig. "And don't worry, when you bring me coffee, I won't let anybody say anything bad about you either."

Emily had procrastinated for as long as possible, but she was out of time. She needed lines on her field. With a gut full of dread, she approached Larry at the beginning of lunch. He was mopping in the conference room. "Excuse me, Larry? I was wondering if you could put some chalk lines on the softball field?"

He stopped mopping and looked at her. After a long silence, he nodded and began to push his bucket away.

"Do you need the measurements or anything?"

He stopped and turned back toward her. "Who do you think lined the field for the last softball team?"

"I don't know. You?"

He nodded. "You can leave a diagram in my mailbox if it makes you feel better, but I doubt much has changed. Most things don't." And then he turned and wheeled away again, leaving her baffled. *What a strange man.*

As she walked by the gym on her way back to her classroom, she had the urge to pop in for lunch duty. Which was weird, as it wasn't her turn. That's a little like going to have a tooth drilled when one doesn't have a cavity. Still, she obeyed the nudge, just in case it was the Holy Spirit giving it.

At first, it appeared there was no reason for her to be there, and both the math teacher and the art teacher expressed their horror at her decision. "Well, if you're going to be here, you mind if I take off?" the art teacher asked.

"Sure, go ahead."

Dominic swore under his breath. Emily looked at him. "Just wish I'd thought to ask first," he said.

"Ah. How goes the job search?"

"Shh!" he said, much louder than she had asked the question. Then he whispered, "It's good. I've had several interviews."

"Mr. Hogan lets you skip school for interviews?"

"He thinks my mother's ill."

Emily took a few steps away from him, suddenly thinking maybe the island should go back to the math teacher resumé pool.

"What did you just say?" DeAnna cried out, interrupting Emily's thoughts. No one was anywhere near DeAnna, so Emily didn't know whom she was talking to. "You wanna say something, say it to my face!" she cried in the general direction of the popular table.

Blake spoke up. "We didn't say anything about you, Anderson. Just mind your own business."

"I heard what you said, Blake!" DeAnna cried, standing up, her shoulders high and squared.

"Then why did you ask?" Blake asked, and several of his cronies laughed. Emily began walking toward DeAnna, not sure what she was going to do when she got there.

But DeAnna was headed in the other direction, toward Blake. "You don't know anything about me or my family," she cried, "and at least I'm not a ..." As she commented on Juniper's virtue, she pushed her in the back.

Juniper stood and whirled around. "Are you kidding me?" she shrieked. "Did you seriously just put your filthy hands on me?"

"Yeah, I did! What are you going to do about it? Have me arrested?" She called her the same name again and looked like she was going to push her again, but Dominic had arrived on the scene and stepped between them. Emily was suddenly embarrassed that she was standing frozen to her spot, and headed toward the fray.

"You're crazy," Blake said to her. "Bojack is going to prison where he belongs."

"He wasn't in any trouble until *her* father started it!" DeAnna cried, managing to sound both threatening and on the verge of tears.

"Oh, will you get a life?" Juniper said. "Get away from me. Go take a shower."

"Juniper!" Emily said. "Enough! DeAnna! Mr. Hogan's office *right now*."

DeAnna turned her head slowly to look at Emily and then said sibilantly, "Make me."

Emily was at a loss. She wanted to drag the child out of the room, but of course she couldn't touch her. She knew Mr. Hogan likely wasn't even in the building. "Fine," she said. "Everyone else, out." She looked at them. "I'm serious. Out. Right now. Leave your trays. Go stand in the hallway."

No one moved.

"Are you nuts?" Dominic asked.

"I said, *now!*" Emily said with more volume.

"Come on, guys," Thomas said. "Let's go."

The students got up and filed out of the gym. Finally, the door swung softly shut behind them, and Emily looked at DeAnna. "Show's over, DeAnna. Not sure what you were trying to prove, but your audience is gone."

DeAnna burst into tears and fled toward the locker room. "You can go let the other kids back in," Emily said to Dominic. "I'll go after her." She followed DeAnna into the locker room in time to hear the outer door click shut. She followed her outside into the bright early spring sunshine and had to shield her eyes as she looked around the parking lot for her. Finally, she saw her running toward the woods. Regretting her pumps, she took off in pursuit.

But when Emily reached the edge of the wood, DeAnna was long gone. Having no idea which direction to pursue her in, Emily trudged back into school.

"What on earth did that accomplish?" Dominic asked when he saw her.

"I didn't hear you having any better ideas," Emily said. "I just thought we needed to separate her and Juniper, and I didn't know how else to do it."

Chapter 31

Emily wasn't shocked when DeAnna didn't show up to practice that day. When she got home, she called DeAnna's mom, who didn't answer the phone. She tried again every half hour until someone picked up.

"What?" a woman snapped.

"Hi, this is Emily Morse, DeAnna's teacher and softball coach. Is this Melinda?"

A grunt.

"I am calling because DeAnna missed practice today. Is she available to speak with me?"

"She's quittin' softball."

"Oh." Emily tried to think fast. "Well, I wish that wasn't the case. Can I ask why?"

"I told her to. We can't afford it."

Emily knew this already. She was the one who had bought the child cleats and a glove. She felt self-righteousness rising up in her chest and tried to kick it out. "Well, I think that everything's been paid for by this p—"

"You goin' clee-ah to Buckfield tomorra?"

"We are."

"So you're gonna stop for lunch. Every kid's gonna get McDonald's or somethin'. We can't be eatin' out meals every softball game. I told her she had to quit and that's final."

"Mrs. Anderson—"

"Name's not Anderson."

"Sorry, Melinda, I wouldn't let DeAnna go without. If she wants to stay on the team, I'll make sure she gets a cheeseburger when we stop. If she's interested, please tell her to be in the ferry line by 6:30." Emily hung up, feeling shaken and a little sick to her stomach. She wasn't sure she'd handled that well, but the woman's rudeness had taken her by surprise.

As Emily fed the cats and then made herself a sandwich, she thought about what DeAnna's mom had said. Of course that would be a hardship, having to give a kid money for every away game. She wondered why she'd never realized that before.

DeAnna wasn't at the ferry terminal at 6:30, but she showed up fifteen minutes later. Emily gave her a big smile, but DeAnna didn't return it. She looked as though she'd rather be anywhere else.

The rest of the girls were very excited. She was surprised at how chatty they could be that early in the morning. The baseball team was far less enthusiastic, as were the few parents who were making the trip.

It was a long bus ride to Buckfield, and Emily wished she was allowed to ride with one of the parents. *I'm a volunteer. Maybe I can.* On several occasions Emily thought she might have to ask the bus driver to pull over so she could be sick. It was the thought of how embarrassing that would be that kept her from throwing up. But, as they neared their destination via the curviest roads in all of America, and the boys all started changing into their cleats, the smell of it pushed her over the edge. She couldn't take it. She stood to lower her window, but it was stuck. Because the bus was at least a hundred years old. She leaned forward and began to wrestle with the window in front of her. MacKenzie looked up at her. "Car sick?" Emily nodded. "Want some help?" Emily nodded again. MacKenzie stood and deftly lowered the window, as if it wasn't a difficult thing to do, and Emily stuck her face out the window. The cold air was bracing and after a single breath of it, she felt better.

"Thank you," she said to MacKenzie.

"You're welcome. Not used to bus rides?"

"Not used to six-hour bus rides."

MacKenzie laughed. "Well, you will be soon."

The gross mismatch in skill was evident even during warmups. Buckfield was just wrapping up their batting practice when Piercehaven arrived, and Emily was dismayed to see the girls thumping the ball all over the field.

"I can't believe it," Juniper said. "I'm actually nervous."

Emily smiled at her. "You, my dear, are going to be wonderful. I've got lots of worries right now, but you're not one of them."

Emily took her girls through a warmup and then, before she was ready, it was time to shake hands with the umps. At that moment, for the first time, she realized she needed team captains. And she had no idea which girls that should be. Without giving it any thought, she yelled, "MacKenzie and Ava! Come here!" The girls, each of them looking shocked to be called, ran toward home plate and began shaking the Buckfield girls' hands.

Then it was time. MacKenzie was up to bat. Though Emily had worked exhaustively on bunting with her, because she thought maybe that was the only way she'd get anyone on base, ever, she wanted to let her at least *try* to hit the ball her first time up.

But it wasn't meant to be. The Buckfield girl was *fast*. And accurate. MacKenzie struck out in three pitches. Without swinging.

"That's OK, MacKenzie, good try," Emily called out, clapping. "Here we go, Hailey, let's get some swings in."

MacKenzie returned to the bench and then ran over near Emily. "Sorry, Coach. She was just so *fast*!"

Emily nodded. "That's OK. Is she as fast as Juniper?"

MacKenzie nodded. "I think so. Maybe even faster. Can I try to bunt next time?"

Emily laughed. "You sure can."

Hailey struck out in three pitches.

Then so did Ava.

And it was the Panthers' turn to play defense.

The Buckfield coach had no such qualms about having his lead-off batter bunt. She laid down a perfect ball right up the third base line. By the time Ava got to it, the girl had already made it to first. Ava threw it anyway. Right out over Jasmine's head. The bunter advanced to second.

"Ava!" Emily called. "Use your head. Don't throw it unless there's a chance of getting her out, OK?"

Ava nodded eagerly. The next time it was hit to her, she had plenty of time to throw it, but didn't. She just threw it to Juniper, who started hollering at her.

"Juniper!" Emily cried. "I'll do the coaching, thank you!" Then, "Ava! You could've gotten her out! Why didn't you throw it?"

"You said not to!"

"No, I didn't! I said use your head! If there's a chance of making the play, throw the ball. If there isn't a chance of making the play, hold onto it. Does that make sense?"

Ava nodded yes, but her eyes said, "No, Coach, I have no idea what you're talking about."

When the bases were loaded—each runner there by error—and Juniper's face had turned the color of pomegranate, Emily said, "It's OK, Juniper! All you can do is your best."

"I know that," Juniper snapped from the mound. Her tone was so disrespectful that Emily's first thought was *I am going to bench her!* But her second thought was *Then what?* She called a timeout and ran out to the mound. Juniper gave her a dirty look. "What?"

"Look at me."

Juniper looked.

"It would be so embarrassing to take you out of this game right now. It would embarrass you, and me, and the whole team, but I will absolutely do it if you *ever* use that tone of voice with me again. Do you hear me?"

Juniper looked sober.

"I *will* do it. Don't test me."

"OK." Apparently, she understood because she remained respectful for the rest of the game. Even as her teammates made error on top of error. Even when she made a perfect play and threw the perfect pass to first base and then watched the ball bounce out of Jasmine's glove. Even when Hailey fielded the ball and threw it to second, when there was no runner on first. Even when MacKenzie made a perfect throw down to second and no one was there to catch it. Even as the score climbed and climbed, she remained stoic.

In the top of the fourth inning, it was finally MacKenzie's turn to bat again. Emily gave her the bunt sign. And even though Emily had incredible faith in this child, she was still amazed when MacKenzie dropped the ball right in front of her and then took off. The Buckfield catcher was no slouch and quickly fielded and fired it, but MacKenzie had wheels, and she beat out the throw. The Piercehaven bench and all six fans went crazy. *We have a base runner.*

She stayed there, on first, as her teammates struck out. *But still. We had a base runner.*

In the fifth inning, Hannah hit the ball to centerfield and the Panthers erupted in cheers again, but the Buckfield centerfielder caught it with minimum effort and the Panthers deflated like a popped balloon.

By the fifth inning, Emily knew why they called it the mercy rule. The score was 26 to nothing, and it was time to go home.

She went through the line high-fiving all the Buckfield players and shook the Buckfield coach's hand. He grabbed it and held it till she looked at him. "Nice job, Coach. You guys look a *lot* better than I expected. Good luck this season." His earnestness left her speechless. She just nodded and smiled foolishly. Walking back to the bus, she realized he was probably just talking about Juniper and MacKenzie, who *had* been pretty amazing, but then she decided it didn't matter what he'd meant. Another coach, a *real* coach, had treated her like an equal—she'd take it.

They got on the bus before the boys' team, affording Emily a quick opportunity. "Guys, listen up. You did a great job. I know it doesn't feel like it, but you did. The Buckfield coach even just praised you. I'm very proud of you. We got killed, and that's OK. Not every team we play will be Buckfield. These guys were good. So, relax and try to enjoy the ride home, OK?"

When they stopped at Burger King, the team filed off the bus. DeAnna stopped beside Emily's seat and held her hand out. Emily didn't understand. "What?" she said, not unkindly.

"My mom said you were going to give me money."

"Oh." Emily was disgusted and defensive, but she said, "I'll be right behind you in line. You just order first, and then I'll take care of it." DeAnna looked disappointed and Emily wondered if she'd actually wanted the cash more than she wanted food.

But then her order made Emily think she did indeed want food. She ordered a large double Whopper meal, a milkshake, and two apple pies. And Emily, thinking next time she'd lay down some pre-order parameters, handed the woman her debit card.

As Emily stood waiting to get back on the bus, holding her salad and bottled water in hand (she'd wanted a few apple pies herself, but figured she should set a good example), Juniper whispered to her, "I don't know why you even let her on the team, let alone buy her supper."

Emily didn't need to ask whom she meant. "Jesus loved that child enough to be crucified for her," she whispered back. "The least I can do is buy her a Whopper."

Chapter 32

Emily decided to give the girls a few days off during April vacation, despite many exclaims of "We never got days off during basketball vacations!" The truth was, she wanted a few days off herself. And she thought a few practices wouldn't make a big difference against Richmond, who was their opponent for the week.

Richmond and Buckfield took turns being the best team in the league, and Emily wished they didn't have to play Richmond quite yet. She'd rather they get in a few games against the less talented teams first.

Still, the schedule was the schedule, so she prayed for rain.

It didn't come.

So on Wednesday afternoon, her team gathered at the field after three days off. Emily watched Sydney Hopkins climb out of her dad's brand-new pickup truck and walk toward the field. Then she watched PeeWee climb out after her and follow her toward Emily. Emily's stomach tightened. She had never had a good encounter with PeeWee.

This one would be no different. "I'd like to talk to you about Sydney's playing time."

Emily had the urge to laugh, but didn't. "We've only played one game. Everyone will get to play."

As if she hadn't even spoken, he said, "Sydney says she only played in one inning at Buckfield."

Emily frowned. She was pretty sure that wasn't true. She would have bet she played in two.

"I've got seventeen girls, Mr. Hopkins. And we only played five innings."

"And whose fault is that?"

What? What is he talking about? "As I said, everyone will get to play. Now, if you'll excuse me." Emily made a beeline for MacKenzie, as if she had some burning instructions to convey, though she had absolutely nothing to say.

MacKenzie did have something to say. "Are Ava and I still captains?"

Shoot. Emily hadn't thought about captains since she'd flung the names out at the last game. "Yes, you are." Emily thought she saw disappointment flash across MacKenzie's face. "What, you don't want to be captain?"

"Well, I do, but I think Hailey's mad. And Juniper too."

"All right. I'll deal with that. You just keep doing what you're doing."

When Emily did call for captains, and named those two girls specifically, she paid close attention to Hailey and Juniper. Hailey stood just in front of their bench, her hands on her hips, staring at the pre-game conference. There did appear to be a problem brewing there. Juniper was flirting with some boys in the crowd. No problem there.

Juniper held Richmond scoreless in the first inning, with no help from her teammates. They got two runners on, but Juniper managed to strike three girls out. Emily shuddered to think what this season might have looked like had Juniper never shown up against her will.

It might have been Emily's imagination, but she thought the Richmond pitcher was a little slower than Buckfield's. But she was still no slouch. She still struck out Piercehaven's first three batters. Despite this, the Piercehavan crowd was very supportive and cheered the girls on as they stood in the batter's box and as they walked back to the bench. There were dozens of people there, many of them standing, and still more sitting in folding chairs all along the third base line. Emily couldn't believe it: they had fans.

Hannah led off the second inning with a triple and the crowd went nuts. People even blew their car horns.

Hannah stood on third base, catching her breath, and absolutely beaming. "Nice hit," Emily said. "Now, take a big lead and if the pitch goes wild, you're going home."

Hannah's eyes grew wide. "I'll never make it."

"You might not. But you might score."

Hannah shook her head. "Miss M, I'm slow. I'll never make it."

"You do what I tell you to do. Now take a lead."

The Richmond pitcher released. Hannah took a big lead. The catcher ignored her and threw the ball back to the mound. Emily wasn't surprised. Hannah didn't look like much of a threat. Emily gave Chloe the bunt sign. Not because she wanted her to bunt, but because she was almost certain she would miss.

The Richmond pitcher wound up, Chloe squared up, the pitcher released, Chloe reached for the pitch, missed it wildly, and the ball zipped past the catcher. "Go!" Emily screamed, her own volume surprising her. Hannah went.

"She's going!" the Richmond coach called, sounding surprised, and maybe a little amused.

The catcher picked up speed, but Emily hoped it would be too late. The catcher grabbed the ball and flipped it behind her toward the pitcher, who arrived to home plate at exactly the same time as Hannah, who executed the world's gompiest slide into home plate and then just lay there breathing hard.

Everyone looked to the ump, but there was no question to the call. The pitcher hadn't even thought about putting the tag down yet. Still no one made a peep till the umpire stretched out his arms, and then the islanders made more noise than Emily had heard since the state championship basketball game.

It had not been pretty. But Piercehaven had scored a run.

Piercehaven lost to Richmond, 19 to 1, in the fifth inning.

After the game, Jake Jasper approached Emily. "Great job, Coach!"

She tried to keep her smile on the safe side of ridiculous. "Thanks."

"If you ever need someone to coach first base, I'm all yours."

She looked at his pants. "That would be great, but just so you know, you can't coach a base if you're wearing jeans."

He laughed. "Are you serious?"

"I am."

"How do you know that? Did you wear jeans to Buckfield?"

"No. I read the rulebook. Three times."

"OK then. I won't wear jeans tomorrow. Maybe I could get one of those stylish uniforms the girls are wearing."

Emily looked at him quickly to make sure he was joking. She thought he was. "I think windpants or sweats will suffice."

Chapter 33

On Thursday morning, the softball crowd had doubled. *Who is watching the baseball game?* Emily wondered. But then she decided she didn't care. She had long known that softball was the superior sport. The island was just catching up.

Jake Jasper joined her at the bench. "Still OK if I help?"

"Absolutely."

"Great. I won't step on your toes or anything. I just want to help."

"Happy to have it."

"I'm not saying it's a bad idea to have the girls coaching first, but well, I think some of the girls don't quite have a grasp on the rules yet."

She laughed. "That's an understatement."

"You mind if I warm Juniper up? Give MacKenzie's knees a break?"

"No, not at all," Emily said, feeling guilty for not having worried about MacKenzie's knees herself. He trotted off toward his daughter.

The day was bright, clear, and 60 degrees. It finally made sense to be outside. The girls seemed almost giddy going through the warmups. "Well, would you look at that," Emily said to Thomas, "the girls are 0 and 2, and yet they're still having fun."

"Shh," Thomas said playfully, "don't call their attention to it. Hey, Miss M?"

"Yeah?"

"You might not want to let Jake help."

Emily groaned. "Ugh. You're right. I didn't even think of that."

"Yeah, well that's why I'm here."

"Really? I thought you were here because of the team full of girls."

"Well, yeah, that too."

"He's the only parent who's offered to help, and he's probably one of the few who knows anything about softball. You're right, Thomas, but I think I'm going to stand by my decision."

"OK," Thomas said, shaking his head.

"What?" Emily asked, knowing he had more to say.

"Oh, nothing. It's just sometimes I wonder if you *like* conflict."

She chuckled. "I assure you. I don't."

Hailey approached Emily then. "Can I speak to you in private?"

Thomas didn't move.

"Thomas, could you give us a second?"

He made a big show of looking put out, but he did toddle off.

"What's up?" Emily asked, even though she knew exactly what was up.

"Some girls on the team were wondering why we didn't vote for captains?" *Some girls on the team. So,* you.

The truth was: they hadn't voted for captains because Emily had forgotten all about captainhood, but she didn't want to say that. So she said, "I didn't want the captain voting to be a popularity contest, so I just picked them."

"But why *them*?"

Now Emily was annoyed. She loved Hailey very much, but sometimes Hailey could just be so ... *Hailey.* "I would think it would be obvious. And though I don't have to explain myself to you, I will give an explanation to the whole team, OK?"

So before the pre-game conference, Emily called everybody in. "I hear there's been some questions about your captains. So, even though I am not obligated to explain my decisions to you, I'll tell you my thought process on this one." *Even though said thought process took me all of three seconds.* "I picked MacKenzie and Ava because they have been rock steady reliable since day one.

They show up, work hard, do what I ask, and are kind to their teammates. Any questions?"

Emily should've known: the first chance Hailey got, she asked, "Don't I show up, work hard, and do what you say?"

Emily looked at her. "You absolutely do, Hailey. You also spend an awful lot of time thinking about your own glory. Will you please just relax? Just go play the game."

In the first inning, Hailey made contact for the first time in her softball career—Emily thought maybe she'd been energized by anger toward her coach. It technically wasn't a hit; it just took an awkward hop that caused the shortstop to bobble it, and Hailey beat the ball to first.

Ava, up next, fouled off a few pitches, but then Richmond threw a change-up and Ava screwed herself into the ground. Strike three. Two outs.

Hannah was up. Still riding high on yesterday's triple. She watched the first pitch go by. Then she cocked and swung at the second, but it was high, and she fouled it off. Emily gave Hailey the steal sign. The pitcher wound up. "Here comes the change-up!" Emily shouted to Hannah, and then, as the pitcher released, Emily saw Hannah put her weight back on that back foot and wait for the pitch, which was indeed a change-up. And then Hannah drove it right up the middle. But the Richmond centerfielder was no slouch. She scooped it up and cocked to throw it toward home before Hailey had even rounded third. Emily sent her anyway. Hailey did have wheels with those long strides and it looked like she had a chance. And then, inexplicably, because Hailey wasn't a softball player yet and was functioning on mere instinct alone, she dove headfirst toward the catcher's shins at home plate. Emily gasped, watching Hailey's young life flash before her eyes, imagining the sound of Hailey's neck breaking, when the ump made the safe signal and the crowd blew up.

"Hannah, I love you!" Emily hollered over the din, and then jogged over to where Hailey was wiping the dirt of her circa 1980 pinstriped pants. "Hailey, that was some beautiful base running, but please don't ever slide headfirst into home again."

Hailey looked at her blankly.

"Just ... feet first next time. Good job, kiddo," she said, bursting with affection, and patted the top of Hailey's helmet.

Emily jogged back to her spot beside third base and looked at Hannah standing on second. "Two outs, kiddo. You're running on anything. Also, if it goes by her, get here."

Hannah nodded and got down and ready.

Emily snuck a look at the Richmond coach. He didn't look happy.

Juniper stepped up to the plate. Emily hadn't let her hit the day before, as she'd been using a designated hitter in an effort to try to get more girls in the game. Juniper swung at the first pitch, and drove it right at the shortstop, who caught it on one hop. But Hannah, not really sure what was happening, knowing only that her coach had told her to run to third, was bearing down on the shortstop, who looked up at Hannah, confused. She made as if she was going to throw it to first, but then reconsidered, apparently thinking it would be easier to tag Hannah, who was only a foot away, but Hannah, finally sensing the danger she was in, turned around and ran back toward second. The shortstop threw it to second base, narrowly missing Hannah's head and completely missing the second baseman's glove. The ball sailed into the outfield. Hannah, seeing this, turned and resumed her run to third. But Richmond's centerfielder was a pro, had seen the whole debacle coming, and had already recovered the ball and thrown it, with alarming speed, to third. "Get down!"

Emily screamed and brought both her arms down hard and fast as though she were desperately bowing before some third base god. Hannah got down, and miracle of miracles, her cleat smashed into the corner of the base just as the third baseman's glove came down. Tie goes to the runner.

The Richmond coach was furious. "All you had to do was throw it to first!" he screamed. "All we needed was the out!"

Emily saw then, with dismay, that she had put DeAnna next in the lineup. At the time, she'd just been trying to give everyone a chance. Now it seemed as though that hadn't been such a good idea. She had runners on first and third, two outs, and DeAnna at bat. *Shoot*. She gave Juniper the steal sign.

They gave Juniper the base. And DeAnna struck out without swinging the bat.

Juniper stormed off the field. When she got to the third base line, she took off her helmet and heaved it underhand at the bench. It hit Thomas, who was looking down at the scorebook, in the shin. "Ow!" he cried.

"You wanna tell me why she's even on the team?" Juniper hollered to no one in particular.

Her father took several quick steps from behind her, grabbed her by her arm, and yanked her around. Emily was grateful it wasn't her throwing arm. He said something Emily couldn't hear, but everyone could hear Juniper's response. "She's not an athlete! She's white trash! And she's making this team a joke!"

Again, Emily knew she should bench Juniper. But she also knew that would be throwing away the game. For someone who didn't care about winning, Emily cared an awful lot about winning.

So because she didn't know how to handle the situation, she let Jake handle it, and soon, a red-faced Juniper was throwing her pre-inning pitches, extra hard, into his glove.

Her fury didn't lend itself well when she threw to the actual batters, however, and she walked in a run. Again, Emily thought, *I should take her out*. Again, Emily had no one else to put in. Both Ava and Hailey could get it over the plate, but they were at third and shortstop right now. They hadn't warmed up, and she'd have to make a scene to pull them from the game to let them warm up now. So, she let things stand, and finally Juniper got them out of that inning having given up only that one run.

As Piercehaven got ready to bat, Emily told Ava to go warm up for pitching. Juniper saw this and tried to sizzle Emily with her eyes.

"Just in case," Emily said to her.

"Just in case *what*?"

When Emily had first said it, she'd meant, "Just in case you keep walking in runs," but now she saw a teaching moment. "Just in case you decide to call one of your teammates white trash again."

Juniper recoiled as if slapped. Then she turned her face toward the field, leaving Emily to think maybe her threat had worked. *Here's hoping she doesn't call my bluff.*

Chapter 34

In the end, Hailey had risked her life sliding headfirst into home for nothing. Richmond beat Piercehaven 12 to 1. But, as Emily made very clear in the post-game huddle, she was greatly encouraged that they had not been mercied. This was the first game they had played all seven innings.

As she headed toward her car, she saw PeeWee approaching, and began to silently pray for divine intervention.

"And this time Sydney only played two innings," he barked.

She stopped walking and flipped open the scorebook. She scanned the page and was dismayed to see Thomas hadn't quite caught all the errors. He hadn't recorded any for Sydney, and Emily could remember at least two. But PeeWee didn't know what the scorebook said. She looked up. "And in those two innings, she had three errors. She got to play, Mr. Hopkins. And she's only a freshman.

Now if you'll excuse me." She tried to walk past him, but he blocked her path. "I'm talking to you. We don't want Jasper coaching our girls. He's done."

Emily looked around, trying to act tougher than she felt. "Who's we?"

"The island. All of us. No one wants Jasper coaching. No one wants Jasper doing anything. And don't think you're all protected just because of the stunt the basketball team pulled for you. This isn't basketball season anymore. We can still get rid of you."

Emily knew by "get rid of you," he meant, "fire," but she feigned confusion. "Are you threatening me? Last I knew such a threat could get you arrested."

PeeWee began to stammer, his face growing redder as he did, and Emily saw James approaching. *Thank you, Father.*

"Everything OK here?" James asked with exaggerated jovialness.

PeeWee didn't answer him. He just stomped away.

"Thank you," Emily said.

"Welcome. So what was all that about?"

"Where have you been?"

"I was watching the baseball game."

"What? Why?"

He laughed. "Did you really need me here? I've got family on the baseball team, and I was—"

"You've got family on the softball team!"

He laughed again and put his arm around her shoulder. "OK, OK, I'll never miss another softball game!"

She looked up at him. "Seriously?"

"No, not seriously." He steered her toward her car and began walking. "Now, what was PeeWee's problem?"

"Oh, he says the island doesn't want Jake Jasper coaching first." As soon as she said the words, she realized "the island" likely included her husband-to-be.

She wasn't wrong. "What?" he said, halting his walk. "Of course we don't! You had Jake Jasper coaching first? Are you crazy?"

Oh my word. Enough already. "No, for the zillionth time, I am not crazy. I needed a first base coach. He offered." *And he even wore windpants.*

"I know, but can't the girls keep doing it? It was good for them."

"No—"

She was going to say more, but he interrupted. "No?"

"No, I'm not going to fire Jake just because everyone on the island thinks everything that happens on the island has to do with windmills."

James took a step away from her. "First of all, you can't fire a volunteer. Second, if he's such a great guy like you say he is, I'm sure he'll understand. Third, having the windmill *foreman* coach first base *is about windmills.*"

James was obviously furious. This made her furious. "I never said he was a great guy. I don't even know him."

"Perfect. Then let's have him coaching our *children* since we don't even know him."

"Oh, for crying out loud, don't pretend this is about the children's safety." And she walked off, leaving the man of her dreams there alone on the side of the road with his fuming.

She drove home, trying not to cry, trying to regain the thrill she'd felt at how well her team had played, before PeeWee Hopkins had so effectively squashed her joy. She started to pray that this stupidity wouldn't affect her relationship with James, but while praying, felt convicted for feeling so angry, and decided she'd rather stay angry than pray. So instead she pulled into her small driveway, walked into her small home that wasn't really hers, locked the door just for good measure, sprinkled some cheese on some tortilla chips, put them in the microwave, and then collapsed on her coach.

When the microwave beeped, she could barely summon the energy to rise. But then the phone rang. She answered, and then tried to make the phone cord reach the microwave.

It was James. "Hi. I'm sorry. I love you. But we need to talk. Can I come over?"

How could she resist?

He was there in five minutes. She hadn't even finished her nachos. "Come in," she called through a full mouth.

He wiggled the doorknob. "I can't!"

She hustled over to unlock the door.

"Why's the door locked?" he asked.

"PeeWee threatened to get rid of me," she said, shutting the door behind him. "I thought I should lock the door."

"Actually, can we leave it open?" he asked.

"No," she said, annoyed with his overdeveloped sense of propriety, "I don't want the cats to get out. And no one can see my door. No one cares whether or not we're sinning."

His jaw clenched, and she knew she'd gone too far. "Sorry. Let me put the cats in the bedroom, and then we'll open the door."

"No, never mind. You're probably right, and I won't stay long. I just wanted to talk to you.

Emily, it's crazy to let the windmills cause *us* to fight. I don't care that much about them. But I do care about you, and I really don't think you should have Jasper coaching."

Emily didn't know what to say. So she just stood there.

"Again, I bet he'll understand. I can even talk to him if you want. But Em …" He paused, as if searching for the words. "You've had an awful lot of controversy around you in the short time you've been here …"

"Yeah?" she goaded him to continue.

"And well, you're going to spend the rest of your life here, right? At least, until I'm dead? I'm sure I'll die first." He laughed, but the joke fell flat. "I just don't want you to be forever thought of as the woman from away who stirs the pot."

Emily waited for him to say more, but he didn't. "None of this pot stirring has been my fault, James."

"*I* know that, but impressions and reputations matter more around here than the truth. Jake Jasper is going to leave as soon as those windmills go up. So is your pitcher. So no one will remember that you sided with them. People will just remember who you sided *against*."

"I'm not siding with anyone, James!"

"Emily, you're not listening to me. I just said, perception matters more than facts."

She took a deep breath and tried to focus. No one ever accused her of not listening, and she didn't like it. "OK," she said.

"OK?"

"OK."

"OK, what? What does that mean?"

"It means I'm listening."

James smiled and looked down at the floor, shaking his head. "There is never a dull moment with you around. I think I understand where you're coming from, Em, I really do. But you need to understand where I'm coming from too. I get that you're trying to protect your pitcher, but she won't even be here next year."

"This isn't about my pitcher."

"It isn't?" He couldn't have sounded more doubtful.

It really wasn't. "It really isn't. I just try to do what's right, or what makes the most sense, and I don't think about the ramifications. Sorry. He offered to coach first. I looked at him as a willing person who knew something about softball and I thought it was the perfect plan. I didn't realize that I had to be a politician in order to be a softball coach."

"I think, Emily, that as long as you're a teacher, you're a politician. So either get used to it or find another line of work. I'm going to go, but can I come back later to take you to dinner?" He stepped closer and kissed her on the top of the head.

"Won't we make a political statement if we go to The Big Dipper?"

He groaned. "You're right. But if we go to the other restaurant, where we never go, people will think that's a statement too."

She smiled and took his hand. "So what? We fast?"

He laughed. "Let's get a pizza to go. Then we can park by the ocean and have a picnic in the truck. We'll stare out at the water, or read all the anti-windmill signs to each other. It will be romantic."

She laughed. "Have you noticed there are no *pro*-windmill signs?"

"There doesn't need to be. They've already won the war."

Chapter 35

On Saturday, April 29, the Piercehaven Panthers traveled to Temple Academy for a doubleheader. James, saying he needed to fish that day, didn't make the trip. Jake Jasper did. Emily thought about letting him coach. It was an away game—who would know? But PeeWee Hopkins was on the ferry too. So, even though it went against every fiber of her being, she went up to Jake and asked, "Can I speak to you for a second?"

"Sure," he said, following her out onto the deck, "but I know what you're going to say."

"You do?"

"You're going to say, 'Thank you anyway, but you can't coach first today.'"

Emily hated the words even as they came out of his mouth. This was so stupid. He was such an asset. She *wanted* his help. "It wasn't my decision."

He gave her a broad smile. "I know that, and I totally get it. If it weren't for the fact that Juniper is having fun, I'd be tempted to tell them to find another foreman for this job. I'd just a soon get off that rock entirely."

"Juniper's having fun?" Emily didn't even try to hide her surprise.

He chuckled and leaned on the railing, looking out at the water, and the island shrinking in the distance. "She is. I mean, life's not perfect, but the scales are tilting in her favor. She really likes that boy she's seeing, and she really likes pitching. She probably wouldn't have gotten the start at Mattawooptock."

"I find that hard to believe."

"You wouldn't if you saw the starting pitcher. She's a senior, and she's better. She's got a curveball that makes college recruiters cry. Anyway"—he pushed himself off the railing and stood up straight—"thanks for putting up with her. I know she's not always easy."

Temple was a small Christian school, and Emily could tell from their warmups that this battle was going to be far easier than anything they'd experienced before.

MacKenzie asked if she could lead off with a bunt and stepped up to the left side of the plate. She offered a few times, but the pitcher didn't throw anything she could bunt, and MacKenzie ended up with a walk. Hailey stepped up next and was very patient in the box, also earning a walk. Ava was *not* patient, but still earned a walk. Emily felt much sympathy for the pitcher who looked near tears. Emily silently prayed for her, and then the Temple coach called a timeout and headed out to the mound. Emily didn't hear everything he said, but she did catch, "Stop trying to windmill."

The next pitch she threw, she didn't windmill, but it still sailed over Hannah's head. The tears came then.

"Do you want a sub?" the coach called out, with gentleness.

The pitcher shook her head fervently and turned to scrape dirt into her toe hole.

It was Emily's turn to call a timeout. The ump looked annoyed, so Emily hustled. "If she throws anything remotely hittable, I want you to hit the ball," she said to Hannah.

"Well, yeah, I was planning on it."

"I know, but what I'm saying is, she might make it hard. You might have to swing at a bad pitch, but if you think you can hit it, I want you to try."

Hannah frowned. "You told us never to swing at bad pitches."

Emily didn't want to tell her the real reasoning behind her direction, that a hit, any hit, would likely still get Hannah on base and drive in a run and would take the pressure off the pitcher and give her a chance to emotionally recover. So she said, "A walk will bring in one run. A hit will drive in two."

"Oh!" Hannah's eyes grew wide with understanding, and she stepped back into the box with a renewed motivation. And sure enough, she swung with all her might at the next pitch—and missed. *Shoot.* Maybe that wasn't such a good idea. The Temple coach gave Emily a look of gratitude though, so there was that. On the next pitch, Hannah cocked her weight and then swung and drove the ball directly at the third baseman's glove. As she caught it, Emily screamed at MacKenzie to get back to the bag, but it was too late. The third baseman only had to take two steps to make the double play.

Emily had instructed her cleanup hitter to forgo the RBI and instead hit into a double play. Oops.

To make matters worse, Ava was confused by the whole thing, and hadn't returned to first yet. Hailey, standing on second, was screaming at her to return to first, but Ava stood frozen. The first baseman was screaming at the third baseman, but she too was flummoxed. Finally, she threw it, but it was a terrible throw, and Ava made it back to first safely while Hailey advanced to third. *This is like* The Bad News Bears, Emily thought, not for the last time that season. She also thought, *Sure would've been helpful to have a first base coach there for that.* She was willing to bet Jake was thinking the same thing.

Juniper was up, and without being told to, laid down a bunt and easily made it to first, bringing Hailey in for their first run. Emily wouldn't have told her to bunt with two outs, but Juniper made the safe bet that they wouldn't be able to field the ball.

Sara was up next and looked to Emily for guidance. "Be patient," Emily said. "Don't swing unless it's a strike." She was done helping the pitcher. She'd learned her lesson.

Sara was patient and got the walk, loading the bases again. Chloe was up next and also walked. Another run walked in. But Jasmine was up next, and her strike zone was considerably bigger than the rest. When she had two strikes, Emily reminded her to protect the plate, but she either ignored her or didn't know what that meant, and stood there for the third strike.

It was time for defense.

When Juniper struck out their first three batters, Emily felt a little like a bully.

Even more so when Juniper did it again in the second inning.

Heading into the top of the fifth, Juniper still hadn't allowed a single hit, and Piercehaven had eleven runs. Emily didn't know they had that many until Thomas said, "We might actually get to mercy someone else for a change."

They scored another two runs in the fifth, thanks to MacKenzie being hit by a pitch (Emily wasn't sure whether it was on purpose); two errors; and Ava's long hit to centerfield. Now all they had to do was hold them, which Juniper did with ease.

"Congratulations on your no-hitter," Emily said to her. "I'm going to start you again, but I might give Ava a shot later in the game, if we get a good—"

"Why?" Juniper snapped.

"Just in case," Emily said. "You're not invincible. You could get sick or hurt at some point."

She walked off in a sulk.

Emily told Ava to warm up for pitching. "Just in case."

"What about me?" Hailey asked.

Annoyed, Emily said, "You can warm up too."

Chapter 36

Piercehaven sprang out to an early lead in the second game. They seemed far more confident and had loosened up in the batter's box. Ava, Hannah, and Juniper all hit the ball well, and even Chloe made contact. She got on base because of an error, but she didn't know that, and was quite pleased with herself.

In the fourth inning, Emily put Ava on the mound. Juniper sat down in the dugout and crossed her arms. Jake came up behind her, said something inaudible through the fence, and Juniper stood up and uncrossed her arms. *Score one for Dad*, Emily thought.

Ava wasn't a pitcher. Still, Emily willed herself to be patient, and tried to give Ava time to settle in, but after she walked four batters in a row, she looked at Emily and said, "Can I stop now?" So Emily acquiesced and gave Hailey a turn.

Hailey, much to Emily's surprise, did OK. She didn't windmill, and it wasn't fancy, but more than half the pitches were strikes, and Temple started to hit the ball. This gave Piercehaven a chance to do some fielding, which provided them with practice and the crowd with entertainment. Chloe bobbled a ball at second and then threw it between Jasmine's legs at first. Emily scanned her memory and decided that no, she'd never seen that happen before. This little mishap scored Temple two runs. Emily had moved Ava to short when she put Hailey on the mound, so the grounder to third came up and hit Sydney right in the face. Thank God she was wearing a mask. The bases were loaded when one of Temple's more-athletic girls stepped up to the plate. She watched the first pitch go by but then swung at the second and sent it toward deep center. By the time Emily looked, Sara had already turned and run, and though she started early, and though she had wheels, it was clear she wasn't going to get there. *That's going to clear three runs*, Emily thought, *maybe four,* but then Sara dove, her glove outstretched. She sprang back to her feet so fast, Emily didn't even realize she'd caught the ball until she flung it toward second base. Chloe wasn't ready for it, but Hailey saw the whole situation play out and got to second in time to catch Sara's not-quite-accurate throw and tag the bag for the double play. Then she turned and fired to first for the triple play. But Jasmine wasn't expecting the throw, and it sailed past first and out of play. The runner who'd been on third safely returned to third in time. The runner who'd been on first safely returned to first. Still, it had been an incredible play and Emily's mouth hung open. *Sara Crockett. Who would've seen that coming*? Emily scanned the crowd for Sara's mom, but she wasn't there. The parents who were there, however, gave her plenty of love. She remained expressionless, just stood there leaning on her knees, waiting for the next ball. Emily was pretty sure that was the first time the island had ever cheered for Sara Crockett.

Emily let Hailey pitch the rest of the game, and they played all seven innings, finishing with a score of 14 to 5. The Panthers' record moved up to 2 and 3. Not bad.

The baseball game went long, and they had to forgo fast food in order to get back to the ferry on time. Emily expected this to cause plenty of complaints of starvation, but the girls were too happy to notice their hunger. The bus ride sounded like a giggle convention and the ferry ride wasn't much calmer. Emily stepped out on deck just to get a break from it all and found Hailey staring out at the water. "You OK, kiddo?"

"Yep. You were right, Miss M."

"Oh yeah? About what?"

"Softball is fun." She grinned.

"I thought you might think so." Emily leaned on the railing beside her.

"You were also right about something else."

"Oh yeah?"

"I don't think I'm a pitcher."

"I never said you weren't a pitcher."

"I know, but you didn't have to. I'm glad you gave me a chance today, but that is harder than it looks. I think I'd rather just play shortstop. I just thought … I don't know."

"You thought you had to be the best at everything you attempt?" Emily guessed.

Hailey nodded. "Yeah, something like that. I just thought I should do the hardest thing, but now …" She didn't finish her thought aloud.

"You can't do everything in life, Hailey. And people who try to be the best at everything end up not being the best at anything."

Hailey looked thoughtful. "Yeah. That makes sense. I'll just try to be an average softball player then."

Emily laughed. "Perfect. I don't even care if you're below average. I just want you to have fun."

"It sure would be more fun if I could hit the ball."

"You will. I promise."

Chapter 37

At church the next morning, Chloe looked a little out of sorts. Emily assumed it was about softball. Softball was pretty much all she thought about lately, despite needing to pick a wedding date and educate the island's teenagers, so it must be all the girls thought about too, right?

She wedged herself into a seat beside Chloe. "Penny for your thoughts?"

Chloe smiled, but her eyes stayed heavy. "I charge at least a dollar."

"Can't afford that rate. I'm a teacher." Emily elbowed her gently. "Come on, spill it. I'm going to be your aunt soon, you know."

That brightened her eyes. A little. "I'll tell you later."

"Oh, come on! Don't do that to me. Now I'll be worried sick all through the service and won't be able to focus on God."

Chloe feigned disgust and then looked around as if to make sure no one was listening. "I'm just thinking about prom."

"Prom?" Emily said, too loudly.

"Shh!" Chloe scolded.

"Sorry," Emily said, lowering her voice. "But prom? Where did that come from?" Emily didn't even know Piercehaven *had* a prom— though, now that she thought about it, of course they did. They were still a high school, but oh what a Lilliputian affair a Piercehaven prom must be. *A pocket-sized prom*, Emily thought and tried not to snicker at her own joke, which she found hilarious. *And where do they buy dresses?* Her mind flashed back to the tote of gowns in the athletic locker. *Ooooh!* "When is it?"

"June 3."

"Chloe, that's like a month away. Why are you worried about it already?"

Chloe looked at her. "You can't tell."

"OK."

"Promise?"

"Promise."

"I think Thomas is going to ask Juniper."

"What? Won't Juniper be going with Blake?"

"She broke up with him," Chloe said, as if that was old news.

"What? When? I thought she really liked him."

"She might have. But he cheated on her, so she said adiós."

"Cheated on her with whom?" Emily couldn't help it. She was sucked into the drama.

"Some North Haven chick. Don't know. But people are also saying that Blake's parents didn't want him with her anyway, because of the windmills."

Emily put her head in her hands. "The stupid windmills," she said through her fingers.

"Yeah. The stupid windmills," Chloe agreed as Abe called the service to order.

The place was packed. Emily ended up stuck where she was, next to Chloe. Someone had taken her seat next to James. People were sitting on the stairs, and several were standing in the back. Emily wondered what the temperature would be in Abe's basement come July. She thought maybe they should start having outdoor tent revivals instead.

As Abe and others shared some announcements, Emily reflected on how unmemorable her proms had been. Oh sure, she'd gone through the motions, done the makeup and the big hair, spent hours looking for the perfect dress, but she'd never actually gotten to go with a boy she liked, and she couldn't remember actually ever having fun. She didn't think she'd ever even danced at one of those things. She felt a little guilty about not taking Chloe's pain seriously and promised God to be more compassionate. Then she also prayed, "I'm not sure you even want Thomas and Chloe to be an item, God, but if you wouldn't mind, could you have him ask *her* to the prom?" Then she thought that prayer was more likely to be answered if Thomas were a follower of Jesus. "Also, God, could you draw Thomas to you, please? He could sure use you right now."

She wondered briefly why the boys were all so gaga over Juniper. Yes, she was beautiful. But so was Chloe. And Hailey. And a bunch of other girls—including Sara, if one could see beneath all the extra-pale foundation and black eyeliner. But then as she thought about it, she figured it out. Juniper was new blood. All these kids had known each other since preschool. They were sick of each other. It was like dating extended family members. And here comes a girl they've never seen before, a girl with long dark hair and big brown eyes. No wonder. She looked at MacKenzie and Noah, sitting on the stairs holding hands, and smiled. At least one couple was working.

All week long, at school, Emily was tempted to say something to Thomas, but she couldn't think of a way to do so that wouldn't be inappropriate. She wasn't really *supposed* to be getting involved with her students' social lives. But still, she cared about the situation a great deal. She loved them both, and didn't want to see her precious Chloe get hurt.

Chapter 38

Their next games were another Saturday doubleheader, this time at Valley High School. This meant another long bus ride, with Emily too sick to read and almost too sick to even be civil to her athletes. She wondered if maybe this should be her last softball season.

But after a few minutes of breathing fresh Maine forest air, those thoughts fell far behind her. It was finally spring in the northeast, and the temperature was behaving accordingly. Which made it extra strange that Hailey was still wearing her undershirt.

"What's with the long sleeves?"

"Aw, Miss M, I can't stand it. These shirts are so scratchy. I'd rather be hot."

"Oh. Well, maybe we can get some new uniforms for next season."

"Or just let us wear T-shirts? These things are so ugly!"

"Your mom's from Valley, right? Do you have family here?"

"No, not anymore. Do you want me to warm up for pitching?"

"I would like you to, yes, but that doesn't mean you'll have to pitch."

"I know that. Thanks, Coach."

It had been happening since basketball season, but she still wasn't used to being called Coach.

Juniper started off strong, and the Valley girls had a lot of trouble hitting her. Occasionally, they got a piece of it, but it never went anywhere.

Valley's pitcher wasn't fast, but she was accurate. Ava, Juniper, and Hannah hit the ball, but Valley's fielders didn't give them any wiggle room. Their infield was solid, and as Hannah learned at one point, their outfield wasn't bad either. Piercehaven got a couple of runners on, but then left them there.

At the end of the sixth inning, the score was still zero to zero.

"This is crap," Hannah spouted in the dugout. "We ought to be able to hit her. She's not even that fast."

"Well, you've got to hit it somewhere where there *isn't* a player," Hailey said.

"Or hit it over the fence," Hannah said.

Hailey laughed. "Yeah right."

"What, you don't think I can?"

Hailey snapped her gum. "No. I definitely don't think you can hit it over the fence, Hannah."

"Hannah," Emily interrupted, "please don't try to hit it over the fence. If you do, you won't hit the ball at all. Just concentrate on hitting it, and eventually, you'll get on base."

"Yeah, and then what?"

"And then let your teammates hit the ball. Believe in them. You're not the only one who can hit," she said with more conviction than she felt.

There were two outs and no one else on base when Hannah stepped up to the plate. She swung at the first pitch fast and hard, and missed. Emily frowned. "Just hit the ball, Hannah," she said sternly. She knew what Hannah was trying to do, and she didn't like it.

Valley threw the second pitch. It came in straight, right down the middle, and Hannah swung that bat like a punishment. There was a satisfying pop and the ball shot in the other direction, right over the left fielder's head. Hannah just stood there watching it. "Run!" Emily screamed. Hannah ran, still watching the ball as it dropped from its arc. *Wow, that might actually make it*. Down, down it came, hit the top of the fence, and ricocheted behind it. Hannah began to jump up and down. She hadn't even made it to first yet. "Run!" Emily screamed again.

Hannah ran, her chin up and chest out. And Emily wasn't even angry that she hadn't done as she was told. How could she be angry? The kid had hit a homerun. And now they had a lead.

But then it was Valley's turn to bat. And it was the top of their lineup.

The leadoff bunted. MacKenzie came out to field it, but Ava crashed down from third to field it. They each deferred to the other and no one fielded it. By the time MacKenzie picked it up, it was too late. The next batter squared up to bunt, but missed—on purpose, Emily thought—as the runner on first went for second. MacKenzie threw down, a beautiful throw that Hailey actually caught, but the runner was fast and beat it out. Now the batter really did bunt. MacKenzie fielded it, looked at the runner leading off second, looked at first, and decided not to throw. Emily wished she'd gone for the out, but she understood why she hadn't. Valley had two runners on.

The next batter cracked a double into right field. Hannah took off after it with all she had, but by the time the ball made it to home plate, Valley had scored.

Their cleanup bunted, MacKenzie held the ball again, and now the bases were loaded.

"You've got to throw them out, MacKenzie," Juniper snapped, "or this will go on all day."

MacKenzie fired the ball back at her with some extra force.

They had no outs. Emily had no hope. She knew they were going to lose. She tried to hide that knowledge. "The play is at home," Emily shouted. "Throw the ball home!"

The next girl up tried to work Juniper, but Juniper was having none of it. She struck her out. Emily exhaled a breath she didn't know she was holding. "Thank you, Juniper," she called out.

Juniper went right after the next batter too, but this girl was a swinger. She hit the ball to Chloe, who fired it to home, but the ball went way left of where MacKenzie was waiting, and Valley's winning run slid across the plate.

Chapter 39

"What is wrong with you guys?" Juniper shouted at her teammates, who were sitting on the grass behind the dugout. "I realize you guys know nothing about softball, but I do! So listen to me! Look at that team! Just look at them!" She pointed dramatically at the empty field. The Valley team was also off the field, having their own, probably more amicable, team meeting. "They are not better than you! That pitcher is *awful*!"

"Juniper, lower your voice please," Emily said.

"I'm sorry, but she sucks!" Juniper said, lowering her voice one-eighth of a decibel. "You should all be hitting her, for crying out loud. She's floating 'em right down the middle. Hannah hit it over the fence!" she said, as if this was proof that the pitcher was terrible.

"Hey!" Hannah cried in defense.

"OK, Juniper, that's enough," Emily said. "We don't need to be bad-mouthing their pitcher." Emily looked at her team. "I think the point she's trying to make is, some of you aren't hitting her because you think you can't hit her. Ava and Juniper hit off her, and had some bad luck in that the ball went right to defenders, but I doubt their bad luck will hold for a second game. That means they're going to get on base, and they're going to need you all to get them home. You *can* hit off her. I've seen you hit off the batting machine, and that was faster than she is. She's probably not going to walk you, so you've *got to hit the ball*." She looked at them. "I don't know how else to put it."

"Seriously, guys," Juniper added. "I'm not trying to be witchy but—"

"Witchy," DeAnna said, "yeah that's not *exactly* the word I'd use."

"Shut up, *stain*. I'm not talkin' to you."

"Girls!" Emily tried, but Juniper kept on going.

"There's no reason we should be losing to that team. They can't hit me. And only a few of them can bunt off me. If we'd throw them out, they'd stop that too."

MacKenzie gave her a dirty look.

"OK, girls, I think we've done enough bonding. Let's get up and get back out there," Emily said. "Get a drink of water and then let's try to have some fun."

A very different Piercehaven team stepped onto the field for the second game. Emily didn't understand the transformation. Were they angry? Had Juniper stoked their competitive fires? Or were they finally just relaxing into their new sport? Emily decided she didn't care. Whatever it was, it was working.

MacKenzie bunted and got on. So did Juniper. Ava singled. So did Hannah. They were on the board.

DeAnna was up next. She popped up, Juniper tagged up, took off with perfect timing and slid into home just under the tag.

Sara was up next and got her first hit of the season, sending Ava across the plate. The girls were screaming their heads off. It appeared to Emily that they were having great fun.

The girls took the field for defense with a four-run lead. And they seemed intent on not losing it. Valley's lead-off batter sent the ball to Hailey at shortstop, who threw her out at first as if she'd been playing softball all her life. The second batter hit to Sara, who caught it effortlessly. Juniper took care of the third batter. Easy-peasy. Back to the bats.

But the Valley fielders also stepped up their game. They didn't make a single error for the rest of the game. They even threw MacKenzie out the next time she bunted. Piercehaven got several more hits, but those hits did not turn into runs.

Then, in the bottom of the sixth, with the score still 4 to zip, Valley decided to rally. A few more bunts, an error at first, and a double to right field garnered them three runs—with the tying run standing on second.

Juniper didn't flag, though. Despite the many pitches she'd thrown that day, she was still firing fast and hard. She struck out the next two batters, leaving Piercehaven in a nail-biting predicament. "The play's at first!" Emily shouted, hoping she didn't sound as desperate as she felt. But there was no play to be made, because the batter drove it up the third base line, sending in their fourth run.

Juniper got the third out herself with three quick strikes, and walked stoically off the field. Sydney and Chloe came off giggling and chatting, leading Emily to believe they had no idea what the score was. Maybe that was for the best.

"Juniper, Ava, Hannah," Thomas called out the lineup.

Juniper stepped into the box, looking confident. She drove the first pitch up the middle. "Thattagirl!" Emily called out.

Ava hit the ball right to first base, getting herself out, but advancing the go-ahead run to second base.

Hannah popped up to the shortstop, who caught it, and then looked menacingly at Juniper, who remained camped out at second.

Two outs and DeAnna trudged to the plate. Juniper gave Emily a look that said, "And here's why you shouldn't have let her on the team."

Emily called a timeout and trotted down to DeAnna. She put her arm around DeAnna's shoulder, and DeAnna flinched. Emily removed her arm. "You can do this, DeAnna. She's going to throw strikes, so you're going to have to swing. But just be confident. You can hit the ball."

DeAnna stared at her blankly. "Why are you talking to me?"

Emily recoiled, considered taking her out, then thought maybe that's what DeAnna wanted. "Because I don't want you to be nervous."

"I don't care enough to be nervous," she said, and turned back to the plate.

At a complete loss for how to respond, Emily returned to her spot beside third. Juniper was still giving her the same look.

The Valley pitcher fired the ball; DeAnna swung and missed, but there was something different in her swing. It looked—angry. Or at least invested. A glimmer of hope danced across Emily's chest. Just a small one. The Valley pitcher snapped the ball again; DeAnna swung the bat—and connected, shooting a grounder past the second baseman and into right field. Juniper took off, and much to Emily's surprise, so did DeAnna. She beat out the throw from right field to arrive safely at first base, where Kylie Greem, Emily's seventh grade first base coach, greeted her with a hug, which, again to Emily's surprise, DeAnna allowed. *I am a stranger in a strange land*, Emily thought.

Sara struck out, leaving DeAnna on first, but it didn't matter. Ahead one run, Juniper ended the game from the mound—one-two-three, and then the Panthers proceeded to celebrate.

MacKenzie took off her mask and looked at Emily. "It's like we finally beat a real team."

"What?"

"You know, the Christian schools, sometimes it seems like they don't count."

"Because they're Christians?"

MacKenzie giggled. "Of course not. But because they're so small."

"Piercehaven's pretty small too, there, champ. And we are certainly a real team."

Chapter 40

By mid-May, the Piercehaven Panthers' record was 5 and 4. Emily could hardly believe it. They had thumped Camden Christian twice to bring their record over .500. And now they were preparing for what was shaping up to be an insane weekend.

They were scheduled to leave school early Friday morning to catch the ferry to Camden. Then they would take a bus from Camden to Rockland, where they would catch another ferry to Vinalhaven. Emily couldn't get over how absurd this was. She asked several people why they didn't just take a caravan of lobster boats, but no one could answer her.

Piercehaven citizens were excited about the impending islander face-off. Sue at the post office told her she'd be there. "I'm so glad you've started the softball program back up. I used to play, you know. It's so good for those girls. I sure do hope you can handle those Vinalhaven girls. They're a healthy stock!" The owner of the pizza place said he was going too. "I always go in the winter for basketball. Might actually be fun to go in the spring!" Marget mentioned it at the grocery checkout. "I look forward to the games this weekend. I hear Vinalhaven's pretty good this year."

Emily had smiled and said, "So are we."

She wasn't worried about the games so much as at the incredible awkwardness of spending the night in a host home—an awkwardness that no one else seemed to find awkward.

She was worrying about this very thing when Mr. Hogan appeared in her classroom doorway during a sixth period quiz over *A Thousand Splendid Suns*. This was a first, and Emily panicked that it was finally time for her professional observation. Since it hadn't happened in her first eight months of teaching, she had hoped it wasn't going to happen at all.

It wasn't going to happen today either. "Could I speak to you, Miss Morse?"

"Of course."

"Out here."

She stepped into the hallway.

"There's been a bomb threat. We're sending kids home. But we don't want them to panic, so we're not telling the kids. We're trying to contact parents now. We'll be calling kids out of your classroom as their parents become available." And then he was off, leaving her with all her questions still unasked.

"What was that all about?" MacKenzie asked.

Emily stood, still and mute. The kids waited. Finally, she said, "I'm honestly not sure. My understanding is that they're letting school out early."

The class erupted in cheers.

"Does that mean no softball practice?" Lucy asked.

"I don't know," Emily said. "Sorry, Luce, I don't really know anything." She wished Thomas was in the room. He'd know what was going on.

One by one, the kids were called out of the classroom until she was all alone and wondering what to do next. She wandered next door, but Kyle wasn't in his room. She headed toward the office. "You're still here?" Julie snapped.

Emily nodded.

"You were supposed to go home."

"Oh, I didn't know that."

"Mr. Hogan told everybody to go home. I'm on my way out now. I was just waiting for the bomb squad."

"The *bomb squad*?"

Julie looked at her as if she were a particularly pathetic specimen. "Yes. They've got to come from Augusta, so it's a good thing there isn't really a bomb. They're on the ferry now."

"How do you know there isn't any bomb?"

"I don't, I guess. But I highly doubt it. This is just the anti-windmillers blowing smoke."

"Why would protesters put a bomb in a *school*?"

"They didn't put a bomb in the *school*," Julie said, using that golly-you're-dumb tone again. "They put the bomb at the windmill site."

"Oh." Emily said, wondering why they'd cancel school for that. "So why'd we let the kids go early? Wouldn't they be safer here?"

Julie stared at her, apparently appalled. "They don't know how many bombs there are, or how big they are, and we're pretty close to the site here."

"We are?" Emily squinted, trying to summon up a map of Piercehaven in her mind.

"As the crow flies, we are. We're sitting on the backside of Chicken Hill."

"So we're within a mile?"

"Definitely."

"So we'll be able to hear the windmills from here?"

"Oh no, not you too."

Emily decided to go home, but when she walked out of the school, she found James just getting out of his truck in the parking lot. "I thought you were fishing?"

"I was. I heard the news."

"How?"

He smirked. "VHF works without a cell signal."

"So what do you know?"

"I know I'm getting you off this island. Come on, get in the truck."

"What?" She was incredulous, but she got in the truck. "James, do we really need to flee the island? Is it that serious?"

"Serious enough that WindRight pulled their crew off the island"—Emily thought of her pitcher and felt sick—"and the State Police sent their bomb squad. And bomb sniffing dogs. They even sent their bomb robot."

"Bomb robot?"

"You know, the thing they use to disarm the bomb remotely."

"So they found the bomb?"

"I don't know, but I'm not waiting around to find out." They came around the corner then and saw the line at the ferry terminal stretched out more than a quarter of a mile down the road.

"There's got to be a hundred cars there. Is that the whole island?"

"Not yet." James backed up and swung his truck into a driveway.

"Where are we going?"

"To my boat."

"James, you're scaring me."

"Yeah, well, this is kind of a scary situation."

"Why do we think there's a bomb?"

"Not *a* bomb. *Bombs*," he said, over-pronouncing the s. "And we think that because someone called up WindRight and said they had planted bombs at the construction site, and that they were going to blow it all up."

"Bombs that big can't be easy to hide."

James looked at her. "You haven't been up there, have you?" He pulled the truck up to the dock.

"No, I haven't."

"There's so much heavy equipment. Work trailers. Outhouses. The giant windmill towers. Those enormous hundred-foot-long blades." He paused. "In other words, plenty of places to hide a bomb."

They climbed into the launch and were wordless as he rowed out to his mooring.

"Thanks for coming to get me," she said.

"Of course, honey. Now, we can head for the mainland, head for Islesboro, or we can just hang out on the water waiting till it all blows over—"

"Or until it goes bang?"

"Right. I don't think that's going to happen. But I do think it's going to take the police a very long time to clear that whole area. But we can do whatever you want."

"Actually, I'd rather you make that decision," she said, suddenly wishing she'd brought her cats. "My house is far enough away from Chicken Hill, isn't it?"

James scooched down in front of her and took her hands in his. "The only thing that makes sense is that this was done by someone who doesn't want the windmills. The people who are protesting the windmills are people who love this island very much. They're not going to blow up the whole island just to prove a point. They're not going to hurt islanders … well, maybe they'd hurt Travis and the rest of Piercehaven Power, but mostly I think they just wanted to hurt the windmill workers. And maybe not even hurt them. Maybe just scare them."

She looked into his amazing eyes. "This could be the end, huh?"

"You're thinking about Juniper."

She nodded.

"No, I don't think this is the end. The person or people who did this will go to jail, and work will continue." He stood up and looked at his island. "Whether we want it to or not."

Chapter 41

They spent the night at a hotel in Camden, in separate rooms, and Emily lay awake most of the night worrying about her students. Where were they all? Were they scared? What did Juniper think of all this?

In the morning, the bomb threat was all over the local news. Emily learned that school had been canceled. They were supposed to leave for Vinalhaven that morning, and she wondered if the game would be canceled too.

An hour later, the newscaster announced that the bomb squad had declared the site cleared. There had never been any bombs.

James and Emily headed back to the island.

When they got there, she didn't know whom to ask about the games. There was no athletic director. She emailed the baseball coach, who promptly answered that yes, as far as he knew, they still had games to play. She found this a tremendous relief. Even though it meant frantically running around to make the ferry.

When she got to the terminal, she was dismayed to find half her team missing. Those present included: MacKenzie, Hailey, Ava, Sara, Natalie, Kylie, Chloe, DeAnna, and Allie. Everyone else was absent—including Thomas and Juniper. She had enough to field a team, but what kind of team would it be without her first baseman, her best hitter, and her pitcher?

She was on the verge of tears when James came up behind her. "Mind if I come along?"

"I thought you had to fish."

"I should," he said. "But I felt like I was supposed to do this instead."

"Thank you," she said, and meant it.

She started Hailey on the mound and slid Ava over to shortstop. She put Chloe on third, which she knew was ridiculous, but she thought she was the least likely to get hurt there. She did tell her to play deep, right beside her base. She put Allie on second, and Sara on first, which left a gaping wound in centerfield, a wound it didn't take Vinalhaven long to find.

The Vikings pounded Hailey all over the field, and Natalie in center didn't have a chance. Neither did little Kylie in left. Emily was grateful that they didn't hit it to DeAnna in right. Though she was also stunned to see that DeAnna was backing up every single throw to first, which was a good thing, because Sara wasn't catching very many of them. Not because she couldn't catch the ball, but because her teammates couldn't throw it. Unless Vinalhaven hit it to Hailey, they got on base. So despite the fact that Hailey threw mostly strikes, and only walked one girl in the whole game, the whole business was a giant disaster.

Ava hit the ball, and MacKenzie got on with a bunt, but other than that, the Piercehaven batter's box was a dry well. The Panthers fell to the Vikings 18 to 0 and Emily was more upset than she thought she should have been.

Then she was assigned, along with sisters Natalie and Kylie Greem, to spend the night at a garrulous widow's home. Her house was beautiful, and she was very hospitable, but Emily just wasn't in the mood to socialize. And the woman was absolutely fascinated with all the windmill drama happening on Piercehaven.

"Darn near tore this island apart, all that foolishness."

"So you didn't mind the windmills going up here?"

"Oh, I minded, but I didn't want to get all shook up over it either. Though, my Max hasn't been the same since." She looked down at her dog.

"He doesn't like the windmills?" Emily was kind of joking.

"Heavens, no! When they first went up, he would howl all night, talking to the spinning blades, I s'pose. My sister's dog was even worse. They live closer to the site, and the windmills would reflect light through their windows, send that dog tearing all over the house chasing that light. Poor Scooby has gone over the rainbow now, though."

Finally, the gregarious woman left her visitors alone to sleep. For the second night in a row, Emily tossed and turned.

God's mercies are new every morning, but Emily didn't wake up immediately cognizant of that fact. Instead, she woke up desperate for coffee. The kind woman didn't have any, but ran out to the coffeeshop. *Vinalhaven has a coffee shop? Color me jealous!*

Emily was exceptionally grateful when the woman returned with coffee in a tall paper cup, and Emily tried to communicate that appreciativeness. Then she, Natalie, and Kylie got into their host's car and headed toward the field, where she finally saw her new mercies. The field was speckled with far more pinstriped girls than had been there the day before, and there was no mistaking the lithe young woman windmilling to her father.

She leapt out of the car and resisted the urge to give Juniper a bearhug. Instead she approached Jake.

"Good morning!" Jake said.

"Morning!"

"Sorry we missed yesterday. I got called back to the office, and I was in meetings all morning. I didn't think they'd play the game, or I would've left Juniper with someone else—"

"It's OK, it's OK," Emily said.

"No, it's really not. Juniper was furious. Still is furious. But I honestly thought no school meant no game. And yesterday was really crazy. I had a lot on my mind."

"I'm sure you did. You're coming back to Piercehaven, right?"

He gave her a broad grin. "I'll pretend it's me you want, and not my daughter, but yes, that is the plan. They offered me a replacement, but I declined. What's a few death threats when your daughter's finally happy on a softball team?"

Emily smiled gratefully. Then, lest she hurt any feelings, she traveled around the field welcoming everyone else back too. And as the girls kept showing up, so did fans. There were *a lot* of Piercehaveners on Vinalhaven that day. Emily was surprised and touched on behalf of her girls. This was going to be a good day. New mercies indeed.

In the pre-game huddle, Emily made it clear that, under the circumstances, no one was in trouble for missing the game. Then she asked those who had missed the game to thank the ones who hadn't. They all did so, aloud, with some giggles. "We tried," Hailey said. "But now let's do better."

"Yes, let's," Emily said, and sent MacKenzie up to bat.

As the girls settled in in the dugout, Emily overheard DeAnna say, "It wasn't Bojack, you know. He's still in jail."

"I know," Juniper said.

"It wasn't any of my family."

"I believe you."

MacKenzie got on with a bunt, and the crowd went wild. Hailey grounded out to second, and the crowd went just as wild. Emily had no idea they could sound so supportive.

Ava stepped up to the plate and some people seated near the left field line stood up and unfurled a sheet that read "Ava the Slay-ah!" Ava singled, moving MacKenzie to third. Then Hannah drove the first pitch right up the middle, allowing MacKenzie to jog across the plate. The crowd was on their feet. Emily stood there looking at them, wondering why they had shown up in such force.

The Panthers scored three runs that first inning, and took the field feeling pretty confident. But Vinalhaven had no intentions of surrendering. They didn't hit off Juniper the way they had off Hailey—not even close—but they did hit off her. Emily was surprised. Juniper looked a little surprised herself. But the team behind her fielded the ball, with the exception of the grounder that rolled beneath Chloe's glove. They ended the first inning tied at three.

They ended the sixth inning tied at seven. They had to score and then hold the Vikings, or they would go into extra innings.

Allie was up. She hit a blooper over the first baseman's head and then acted as if she'd hit a homerun. *Whatever. We'll take it*. They were at the top of the lineup. The infield collapsed in on MacKenzie. She gave Emily a panicked look. "Just hit the ball," Emily said.

MacKenzie's eyes widened in further panic. She asked the ump for a timeout and then ran to her coach. "Can I still bunt? I think I can beat out the throw."

"No, you cannot bunt with them that close. I want you to swing and drive it down their throats."

"Coach!" MacKenzie said, shocked.

"Take a good swing. Try to hit it, but even if you don't, maybe they'll move back." MacKenzie looked doubtful, but she went back to the plate. And she swung. And missed. Emily clapped her hands. "That's OK, that's OK, get this one."

The defenders didn't back up. *That's so dangerous*, Emily thought. MacKenzie swung and missed again. Two strikes, the coach told his players to back up. *That was a mistake*, Emily thought, and sure enough, MacKenzie laid down the perfect bunt and took off. Emily had told them over and over not to bunt on a third strike, but she also knew that MacKenzie was an incredibly stubborn child. An incredibly stubborn *safe-at-first* child.

Juniper stepped up to the plate, fouled off four pitches, and then hit it directly to the right fielder, who caught it. Allie tagged up and took third. Emily couldn't decide whether to send her home, so her indecision decided for her, and Allie stayed at third. "Shoulda sent her!" someone called from the crowd. *Ah, that's more like it. That's the Piercehaven I know.*

Ava the Slay-a stepped up to bat. She hit a grounder to the shortstop, who fielded it, checked Allie on third, and then threw Ava out. Again Emily held Allie at third, though she felt tremendous pressure from the faceless fan behind her. Allie wasn't fast, and she wasn't a good slider.

So it was two runners on with two outs when Hannah stepped up to bat. She belted it to centerfield, bringing Allie and MacKenzie safely across home plate.

Hailey was up next, and she looked nervous. Emily ran over to her. "No pressure here, kiddo. The work's been done for you. The rest is just cushion." Hailey didn't look convinced and stepped into position. Then she hit a piddly ball down the first base line. She was tagged out before she ever got to the base.

"Don't sweat it, kiddo," Emily called out. "Now we just have to hold them."

Hailey nodded and ran to shortstop.

Juniper threw the first batter out. MacKenzie caught a popup. And it looked like it was almost over. But then a Viking hit a single. And then another Viking hit the ball to Ava, who bobbled it and didn't get the throw off in time. Emily wondered if she was getting an ulcer. With runners on first and second, the next Viking hit it right into the hole between shortstop and third, but Hailey dove to her right, something Emily had never seen her do, and stopped the ball. Then she scrambled to her knees and threw the ball to Ava at third base.

"Tag the bag! Tag the bag!" Emily screamed like a raving lunatic. Ava tagged the bag. The game was over. The correct island had won. And no one had thought about wind turbines or bombs for at least ninety minutes.

Chapter 42

On Monday morning, Emily found a very excited Chloe in her classroom.

"Guess what!" Chloe chirped.

"What?"

"Thomas asked me to go to the prom with him."

Emily was stunned. "Really?"

"Really. I mean, he didn't do it romantically or anything. He just said, 'Hey, you wanna go to prom?'"

"And you said yes?"

"Of course."

"Whom did you go to prom with last year?"

"Thomas."

Emily laughed.

"What?" Chloe asked, looking suspicious.

"Nothing. Just island life is all."

"We've been friends a very long time."

"I see. And how long have you wanted to be more than friends?"

Chloe shrugged. "I don't know. Not sure I do want that."

"Can I ask, Chloe, does your mom mind you hanging out with Thomas?"

Chloe looked confused.

"I mean, because of all the windmill stuff. I have surmised that she's not a big fan of Travis."

"Oh, she *hates* Travis. But she doesn't mind Thomas. She was friends with his mom."

"Interesting. Well, good. Where is Thomas anyway?"

"I don't know. He's here somewhere; he gave me a ride."

Thomas never appeared before class, and then he was late for second period. When he did show up, he wouldn't make eye contact. Emily got the sense that she'd done something horribly wrong, but she couldn't imagine how she'd offended him. He was still behaving strangely during seventh period, when he came back to her room for creative writing.

Even Duke noticed. "Why so quiet, Payne? Windmill stress got you down?"

Emily didn't like his tone, and told him as much. "None of this is Thomas's fault, Duke. He's not putting up windmills."

"No, but he's certainly going to benefit from this island's destruction."

Thomas didn't even flinch at Duke's attack, so Emily let it go. When the bell rang, she said, "Thomas, can you hang on for a second?"

He stopped, but he still didn't look at her.

"Are we OK?"

He gave a fake laugh. "Of course."

"OK, because if I've done something to upset you, I don't know about it."

He didn't say anything.

"And I would want to know about it. So I could apologize."

He finally looked at her but the usual spark in his eyes was replaced by an uncharacteristic sadness. "You didn't do anything."

"OK," Emily said, and then, because she didn't want to give up, she said, "You can talk to me about anything, you know. I will try to help, whatever it is."

"I know," he said, and made a beeline for the door.

He didn't show up to practice either. Emily called Chloe over. "Do you know what's wrong with Thomas?"

"No?" Chloe looked alarmed.

"I don't mean to scare you. I'm sure it has nothing to do with you. But he swears he's not mad at me, but acts like he is. I just want to know what's wrong, so I can help. Even if it's none of my business, I still want to help."

"OK, I'll ask."

The next morning, Chloe came to Emily's room alone again. "How are you doing, Chloe?"

"OK, but you're right, something is up with Thomas. He swears up and down he's not mad at you, but he wouldn't tell me what's going on either."

"OK," Emily said, pushing her chair back from her desk and standing, "where is he?"

"In the gym, I think."

"Let's go get him." Chloe followed her out of the room. Emily looked back at her, "Or if you're embarrassed to be part of this intervention, I can do this alone."

"Don't be weird. I'm not embarrassed."

But Thomas certainly appeared to be. "I really can't talk right now," he said, looking around nervously.

"What? Why?" Emily asked. "You're standing here all by yourself."

Thomas looked at her. "Please," he said gravely, "just leave me alone."

"If I leave you alone, I'm calling your dad. I am genuinely—"

"No, don't call my dad. Fine. I'll come talk to you. Just go to your room." He looked tortured. "Please," he added.

Emily and Chloe returned to Emily's room and waited. But he never showed.

Chloe reappeared after first period though, looking considerably more somber than she had earlier. "OK, he told me what's going on. And I get it. I get why he can't tell you. And I am *begging* you to stay out of it. I am begging you to just trust us."

They stared at each other for a moment. Then Emily said, "No."

"No? You can't trust us?"

"I do trust you. Now you need to trust me. Tell me what's wrong."

"We do trust you. That's *why* we can't tell you. I'm sorry, Miss M, but this will all be over soon." And she was off down the hall.

Thomas skipped his English class altogether, so at lunchtime, Emily wandered down to the gym to see if he was eating. He wasn't there. Emily saw something else interesting, though. A bunch of kids were crowding around Tyler, looking at something on his phone and laughing. Emily snuck up behind them to take a peek. And though she couldn't get a good look, she thought she was seeing two people, one holding the other up, the other appearing unable to hold themselves up. "I'll take that," Emily said, and reached for the phone.

A few kids made dramatic "ooooo" noises, as though Tyler were in big trouble, but most of the kids just scattered silently. Emily saw Chloe looking at her, and she looked as though she was going to be sick. Emily moved the phone closer to her eyes, rewound the video, and pressed play.

Oh no. It was Juniper. Her legs like floppy puppet legs, her mouth hanging open, one hand still clutching a forty, her neck like jello, her head resting on a shoulder that wasn't quite in the frame—and then it was. The shoulder belonged to her first baseman. *You've got to be kidding me*. And then on the heels of that, *This is what Thomas couldn't tell me*. She was struck with a sudden fear that her entire team had been at this party, and she exited out of the video to swipe left and then right. Lots of pictures. A few more videos. Thomas was in one of them. But none of her other girls were featured. Just Juniper and

Jasmine. She looked up at them, and they were looking right at her.

Her first thought was that she needed advice. She wished she had an athletic director. She wished James wasn't out in the middle of the ocean. But then she thought, *I can do this myself. I know what I have to do. I don't have a choice. There's nothing to debate.* But first, she had to review the athletic contract they had all signed.

Trouble was, she'd turned them all into the office, she didn't know where Thomas had gotten a blank copy, and she couldn't exactly ask him right then. For lack of any better options, she went to Kyle's classroom. "Hey, what's the consequence for breaking an athletic contract?"

"What, you mean, here? Nothing!"

"That's not true. The kids all sign a contract that says they won't smoke or drink during the season. What happens if they do?"

He snorted. "And I'm telling you that no matter what they sign, *nothing* happens. Milton used to drink *with* the girls."

"I'm not Milton," she snapped.

"No, indeed you are not. Don't you have a copy of this contract?"

"I do not," she said, embarrassed, "and I don't want to have to ask Julie for a copy, because then she'll want to know why I need it."

He stood up. "I'll go find one."

"Really?"

"I don't know—who are we kicking off the team?"

She scowled at him.

He laughed. "Yeah, I'll go get one. I've figured out how to charm Julie after all these years."

She was skeptical. But she was also grateful. "I'll be in my room."

"OK. But then you've really got to tell me who we're kicking off the team."

Chapter 43

The contract read, very clearly, that student athletes were not allowed to use drugs or alcohol. If they did, they would be suspended for one week for their first offense. A second offense meant removal from the team.

Emily groaned.

Kyle, perched on the edge of her desk, said, "You can still pretend you don't know."

"The whole school saw me watch a video of her completely hammered, hanging off her teammate."

"Well, then right now I'm sure they're coming up with a story. Just accept the story and then move on with your life."

She stood up just as the bell rang. "I can't."

He stood too. "Of course you can't." He headed out of her room.

"Thanks for your help," Emily said, and really meant it. Maybe Kyle wasn't so bad.

Emily tried to focus on her last two classes of the day, in which she had neither Juniper nor Jasmine. She did have Thomas, who did show up for class. He was fairly meek throughout the period, and then stayed after the bell. "I'm sorry, Miss M. I just couldn't tell you. I couldn't be a rat, but I also couldn't lie to you."

"I get it, Thomas," she said, and she almost did get it. "And the whole school knew?"

Thomas shrugged. "Pretty much. Chloe didn't, till I told her, and made her swear on her iPad not to tell you."

"OK, let's get to softball practice then."

When Emily got to the field, the girls were a melancholy bunch. They stood there calmly and quietly watching her get out of her car. She walked over, dropped the equipment by the bench and said, "Jasmine and Juniper, can I talk to you?"

The girls trudged over and looked at her expectantly.

"I adore each of you," Emily said. "I really do. But we can't let this slide. You signed a contract, promising your teammates that you wouldn't drink. You broke that promise. So now I have to suspend you from the softball team for one week."

"Miss Morse!" Jasmine screeched. "That's a bunch of bull! Everybody in that school drinks all the time!"

"Are you saying that more of your teammates were at that party?"

"Well, no."

"Are you saying that more of your teammates have consumed alcohol this season?"

Jasmine looked at the toes of her cleats. "No," she mumbled.

Emily took a big breath. "You made a choice, Jasmine, a choice that has nothing to do with anyone else. You choose to drink alcohol in public—"

She made a loud *pfft* sound. "It wasn't in public."

"Where was it?" Emily asked.

Jasmine shrugged. "At the beach."

"So, *public*. You let someone *film* you."

"Well, I didn't know he was going to show a *teacher*."

"OK, Jasmine," Emily said, her temperature rising, "I'm done talking to you about this, as you are obviously completely unwilling to take responsibility—"

"I wasn't even drunk!"

"What?" Emily said.

"I didn't even drink. I was just there. You can't prove I drank."

"Shut up, Jazz," Juniper said. "You drank."

Jasmine swore at Juniper and then stormed off toward the road.

"Can I still practice?" Juniper asked.

"No, sorry."

"Can I *be* at practice?"

Emily hadn't thought of that. She didn't know the answer, but she guessed, with no athletic director and an invisible principal, it was up to her. "Yes, I think that would be a good idea."

"OK, thanks." She turned toward the bench, took two steps, then stopped and looked back at Emily. "And I'm sorry, Coach."

Emily just nodded and then headed toward the rest of her team.

Hailey met her before she got there. "Can we talk?"

Emily nodded and stopped walking.

"Please don't suspend them. We need to beat Searsport *twice* to make the playoffs."

"Maybe—"

"No, I'm telling you, we *do*. I figured out the Heal points. We beat them twice, we're in. We lose even once, we won't make it. And they're not great, but they're Class C. They're not going to be easy to beat. We *need* Juniper."

"I hear you, Hailey, but I can't ignore this. They made a decision. There have to be consequences."

"Miss M, you don't understand. Everyone drinks. All the time. It's a fact of life. You're not teaching them anything. They're still going to drink when they grow up. They're still going to drink next week."

"I hear you, Hailey, but I've made my decision. Now let's practice."

James stopped by her house later that evening. She hurriedly ran a hand through her thick hair and checked her teeth. Then she sat back down on the couch and tried to act naturally. "Come in!"

"Hey, just wanted to check on you."

"So you heard?"

"I heard. And for what it's worth"—he sat down on the other end of the couch—"I think you made the right call."

"So the island doesn't hate me again?"

"Nah, no one cares about softball."

"I'm not so sure that's true. You didn't see them that second day at Vinalhaven. They were great."

"Who? The fans?" He looked shocked.

"Yes, the fans. You know, those people who actually *go* to softball games?"

He gave her a sideways look. "I went to the first Vinalhaven game."

"Yes, yes, you did. Thank you."

"Hey," he said, fishing his phone out of his pocket, "I wanted to show you something."

She saw him scrolling through videos. "I've already seen it."

He shook his head. "Not that. *This*." He handed her the phone. Three girls were on the softball field. MacKenzie, *not* in her gear, was sitting on a bucket behind home plate. Hailey and Juniper were on the mound.

"What are they doing?" Emily asked.

"Just watch."

Hailey went through a windmill windup and fired the ball to MacKenzie. Then the video stopped. Emily looked up at him. "She's windmilling?"

"Yeah, I drove by earlier to see if you were still there, and you weren't, but they were. I watched for a few minutes. Juniper was teaching her to throw. I just videoed a few seconds of it to show you, not because I'm creepy."

"She thinks she's going to teach Hailey to windmill in four days?" Emily asked, skeptical.

"She thinks she's going to try."

Chapter 44

On Wednesday morning, Hailey, MacKenzie, and Juniper walked into school together a few minutes late. They were all wearing sweatpants and messy ponytails.

Well, isn't that suspicious? Emily played dumb at practice that day (which Juniper did attend and Jasmine did not) and then she drove James's truck—to remain incognito—back by the field an hour later. They were still out there, and the pitch Hailey threw as Emily drove by looked pretty solid.

On Thursday, during creative writing class, Hailey winced while getting out of her chair.

"Sore?" Emily asked nonchalantly.

"I'm OK," Hailey said. "My arm's a little sore, but it's no biggie."

Emily waited for her to look up at her. When she did, Emily said, seriously, "Don't hurt yourself over softball. You only get one body. Softball isn't worth abusing it."

Hailey looked surprised. "OK, Miss M. I won't."

But they were there again on Thursday night, and came to school in sweats again on Friday.

At Friday's practice, Hailey came clean—partially. "Miss M? I was wondering if I could pitch batting practice. I think I can windmill tomorrow, and I'd like to practice on some real batters."

"You think you can windmill?" Emily played it cool.

MacKenzie stood nearby, expressionless, but focused on the conversation. Juniper stood near the bench, out of earshot, looking nervous.

"Yeah," Hailey said. "I've been practicing. It's a little wild, but not crazy wild. I don't throw it over the backstop or anything."

"You shouldn't have been practicing windmilling without proper form. You could hurt yourself."

"I've got proper form."

"How do you know that?"

"YouTube."

Emily took a step closer to Hailey and lowered her voice. "I know she's been helping you. What I don't know is why that's a secret."

Hailey looked surprised, and then shrugged. "She thought she wasn't allowed to practice."

"But you guys have been doing it outside of practice hours, so it must be more than that."

Hailey looked at Juniper and then back at Emily. "I think that she cares, but that she doesn't want anyone to know that she cares."

Emily nodded. "Fair enough. Let's give it a try. MacKenzie, get your gear on."

Hailey was not very good at windmilling. But she was miles better than Emily thought she'd be and she was far better than any other option they had. The young woman was truly an athlete. She looked miserable, grunted every time she released, and frequently rolled it across the plate—but still, it was something.

And her teammates were very supportive of her, especially MacKenzie, who had to work extra hard to keep the ball in front of her—by the end of practice, she was filthy. Emily had Ava put on the catching gear so that MacKenzie could get some swings in. After ten minutes of that, Ava ripped off her mask and exclaimed, "This sucks!"

Emily cocked an eyebrow. "Catching?"

"Yes! Catching! Who would ever want to be a catcher?"

"I love catching!" MacKenzie chirped.

Emily knelt down to help Ava out of the gear. "I've been meaning to tell you," Ava said. "Since tomorrow might be our last games, I want to say thank you for this."

Emily looked up at her. "For what?"

"For giving me softball my senior year. I was never any good at basketball, never even really liked it, and though I'm not great at softball, at least I'm kinda good? You know?"

Emily smiled and put her hand on Ava's back. "You, my dear, *are* great at softball. And don't let anyone tell you any different. I don't even want to think about what this season would have been like without you."

Ava beamed. "Maybe I could come back next year and help you? Maybe I could coach first?"

"Aren't you going to college?"

Ava shrugged. "I didn't apply anywhere."

"Well, you've still got time to apply for the community colleges. I could help you with the process? Presque Isle has a softball team."

Her eyes lit up. "Really?"

"Yep, and if you went there, you could major in windmill technology."

Ava laughed. "That might not even be a bad plan."

Chapter 45

Searsport had a not-very-good softball team, but they were a Class C school, which made them worth more Heal points. Emily had taken Hailey's math as gospel and trusted her that a pair of wins today would get them into the playoffs.

Just the idea of playoffs made her head spin. *Playoffs*? She'd never even thought it possible. And she was well aware that it hadn't been possible before Juniper showed up. But now Juniper was in street clothes, and Hailey was fixedly watching the Searsport team take batting practice, her jaw clenched. Emily felt a pang of anger toward Juniper, for putting Hailey in this situation. But then Juniper asked Emily if she could please stand with the team, and the anger dissipated.

The Piercehaven fans showed up in force at Searsport. The ferry had been packed. Many of them seemed to know what was at stake.

Perhaps Hailey wasn't the only islander who understood Heal point math.

When the Searsport pitcher stepped onto the mound, the crowd began screaming in support of MacKenzie, and someone began ringing a cowbell, a sound that both embarrassed Emily mightily and increased her heart rate in a pleasant way. MacKenzie bunted left-handed and then took off, her little legs moving so fast they looked blurry. But she was the only runner to get on base that inning.

Hailey walked the first batter, which made Emily's heart crack for her, but Hailey looked at Emily and gave her a small smile that said, "I'm OK."

And she was OK. The second batter worked her, but Hailey stuck with it, and forced her to swing. Ava deftly made the play to first, and Hannah caught the ball, a fact that, if Emily was honest, surprised her. Searsport's only runner advanced to second.

Their third batter sent the ball into left field, toward a terrified Lucy. As Lucy stared at the sky, a cry of "I got it!" surprised Emily and she looked over to see Sara coming from center. She dove, both arms outstretched, and caught the ball just before it hit the ground.

"Back!" the Searsport coach shouted. The runner turned and headed back toward second. Sara leapt to her feet and gunned it toward Chloe, who miraculously caught it. Sara and Chloe for the double play.

As the girls trotted back to the dugout, Emily overheard Lucy ask Sara, "How do you do that?"

Sara shrugged. "I can tell where the ball is going as soon as someone hits it. Then I just start running."

Sara led off the second inning, and struck out, but she either didn't care or hid her emotions marvelously. Chloe was up next, and grounded out to first. Then Victoria struck out. Emily resisted the urge to hang her head.

In the third inning, Piercehaven made a few errors and Searsport rallied to three runs, but then Hailey called a timeout. Emily didn't know what she said, but the infield settled down after that and got their third out.

In the top of the fourth, Hannah sent one into right field, sending Hailey home and Ava to third base. *Finally,* Emily thought. Then Sara grounded out, but in doing so, sent Ava home. The Panthers' tying run was on second, and Chloe was up to bat.

She struck out.

Tying run still on second. Two outs.

Emily thought about putting in a pinch runner for Hannah, but didn't want to insult her—she'd likely remember such a slight for the rest of her life. *Plus—Hannah may be slow, but at least she knows the rules of base running, sort of. That's more than I can say for the girls on my bench.*

Victoria stepped up to bat, and hit the ball directly to the first baseman. *Thank God I didn't do that to Hannah for nothing.*

So Piercehaven took the field for the bottom of the fourth still down by one run. They stayed down until the top of the seventh, when, miracle of miracles, Sydney Hopkins got on base. Lucy was up next, and hit a fielder's choice. The fielder chose first, and Sydney advanced to second. Then a wild pitch brought her to third. DeAnna's count was 2 and 0. Emily was hoping she'd walk, and it appeared DeAnna was hoping for the same, as she stood there until the count was full.

"Time to swing the bat, kiddo," Emily said.

DeAnna swung the bat. She cracked a line drive right at the pitcher, who didn't catch it, but did knock it down. The pitcher scooped the ball up and turned to throw it to first. Emily sent Sydney. But then the pitcher turned and threw it to the catcher, who was straddling home plate, waiting for the ball. Sydney made a clumsy slide attempt, and the catcher easily tagged her out.

"Why did you send her?" PeeWee Hopkins screamed from the crowd. Emily's whole back broke out in gooseflesh, and she forced herself to breathe. She felt every eye on the island boring holes into her back. "That was terrible! Absolutely terrible!" PeeWee screamed. *Breathe. Just breathe.* The truth was, no one as angry with her as she was with herself. She thought she'd probably just blown their chance at playoffs. She'd been faked out by a high school pitcher. And she couldn't believe she'd been so stupid.

But she still had DeAnna on first. DeAnna, who was either a slow runner or a lazy one. DeAnna, who didn't know the rules of base running. "Two outs," Emily called out to her. "You're running on anything!" DeAnna nodded as if she understood. Emily didn't know if she did. She really wished Jake Jasper was coaching first, not seventh grader Kylie. "Juniper!" Emily snapped. "Go coach first!" In a flash, Juniper had a batting helmet on and was standing beside first. Emily thanked God she hadn't chosen to wear jeans.

MacKenzie stepped up to bat and looked at Emily, who shook her head, which both of them understood to mean, "You can't bunt." MacKenzie nodded, and then worked the pitcher for the walk, but it wasn't happening.

ROBIN MERRILL

MacKenzie struck out with a sloppy swing—a swing so sloppy it confused the catcher, who missed the ball entirely. MacKenzie took off. "Run!" Juniper screamed at DeAnna, who ran. Faster than she'd run all season. The rattled catcher recovered the ball and fired it to first, but her throw was off, and MacKenzie turned toward second. Now both she and Juniper were screaming at DeAnna to run. DeAnna ran. All the way to third base, where she arrived—winded and *smiling*.

The crowd was ballistic behind Emily. *Maybe they'll forgive me.* Then she looked at her next batter: Hailey was white as a sheet. Emily called a timeout. "Look at me," she said.

Hailey looked at her. "Coach, I am a terrible hitter. You know—"

"Listen to me. And hear what I say. This *does not matter*. This is a game. You are going to go on to have a full life and what happens here does not matter. It does not matter if you hit a homerun or strike out. You will still be amazing. You will still be loved. So just relax and do your best."

Hailey didn't look entirely convinced, but she did look a little more relaxed. She looked at the first strike, but then she swung at the second—and shot it right up the middle. DeAnna lazily crossed home plate, and Hailey stood on first base with both arms in the air. Then, Piercehaven's first base coach wrapped her arms around Hailey's waist, picked her up off the ground, gave her a good shake, and set her back down. Emily wasn't sure if that was legal, but the umps didn't protest.

Ava was up to bat. She seemingly effortlessly singled to left field, advancing the go-ahead runner to third. Emily reminded them that there were two outs, but they could barely hear her over the roar of the crowd. Piercehaven fans outnumbered Searsport fans three to one.

Hannah stepped up to bat and turned the first pitch into a stand-up triple, and Emily's coaching mistake was buried beneath the joy of taking one step closer to playoffs. The giddy Panthers held their opponent in the bottom of the seventh. They had beaten Searsport. One more game to go.

The second game required far less nail-biting. It seemed as though Searsport had grown tired of softball, and was just going through the motions. Though Hailey was obviously growing fatigued, and though her walks became more and more frequent, even walking in two runs in the sixth inning,

Piercehaven still finished victorious with a score of 7 to 4. Emily was certain she had never been so tired.

She didn't even let Hailey get off the field before she wrapped her arms around her. "I am so proud of you, kiddo," she said into her ear. "You just took us to the playoffs."

Chapter 46

After the Searsport wins, it was all prom planning all the time. Even though Hailey got a sports section front page write-up in the *Bangor Daily*, as the "Basketball standout turned pitcher," she was much more interested in her prom plans. She was bringing a senior boy from Vinalhaven, which had Piercehaven boys annoyed and Piercehaven girls jealous.

Emily asked Juniper if she was going to the prom, and Juniper laughed derisively. Emily asked DeAnna the same question, and DeAnna said, "Of course not," implying that it had been a ridiculous question. When Emily asked Sara, Sara told her the prom was a commercialized misogynistic social construct.

But the rest of the girls had either paired off with boys or were going in all-girl gaggles. Sydney had made the trip to Portland for a gown, which she made clear had cost five hundred dollars, but most of the girls had ordered online, and new gowns arrived each day. Julie, to her credit, unpacked the crate of gowns from the athletic locker, steamed them, and hung them in the office. Anyone who wanted to could try one on and/or take one home. Emily wondered if there was a tuxedo crate somewhere too.

Julie asked Emily to chaperone, and Emily declined in a voice that quivered with panic. But when she told James about the offer, he said, "Aw, let's do it. It'll be fun." Apparently, Julie had asked him too, as the girls' basketball coach.

Maybe it wouldn't have been so devastating if the State Police had shown up on an ordinary day, when the students were their usual grumpy selves. But they showed up on the Wednesday of prom week, when boys were scheming about transportation and booze, and girls were planning hair and makeup. They came into Emily's seventh period creative writing class, and, after a perfunctory apology for interrupting, ordered Duke Crockett to come with them.

There were four of them, two in suits and two in uniform, as if Duke were some violent ninja whom one cop couldn't handle. This impressive display of force scared Emily, but not as much as Duke's response scared her. Duke was *never* without a wise guy quip, never without a mocking gesture, but in that moment, he looked like a very young child, a child who knew he was in an awful lot of trouble—he looked terrified.

Emily couldn't imagine why they'd taken Duke, but after several silent shell-shocked seconds, Thomas volunteered a theory: "He must've been the one who called in the bomb threat."

Emily couldn't believe that, and jumped to his defense. "Duke is a peace-flag-waving hippie. He doesn't even eat meat. He doesn't make bomb threats."

But Thomas stood by his theory. "Miss M, but he didn't actually use bombs. He just made the threats. And I guarantee his mother is loony enough to make him do it. Think about it. What else could they possibly want him for?"

Emily was still in denial. Duke wouldn't be that dumb. Duke didn't care enough about the stupid windmills to be that stupid. Did he?

But after the final bell rang, when a sobbing, shaking Sara showed up at her classroom door, eyes raccooned with smudged eyeliner and tears, and fell into her arms, Emily started to believe it. Duke was in serious trouble.

At lunchtime on Thursday, Hailey came bolting into Emily's classroom. "They just posted the brackets," she said breathlessly.

"What?" Emily had been thinking about Duke and had no idea what Hailey was talking about.

"The playoff schedule. It's online. We're going to Valley."

"Oh!" Emily said, finally understanding, and joining in on, her excitement. "Valley? I thought we were in sixth place. Doesn't that mean we'd play Buckfield?"

"No, the first and second place team get a bye in the first round. So we play third place, which is Valley."

"I'm surprised they're in third place. I mean, they were good, but they weren't great."

"I know. That's why I'm excited. We beat them, Coach!"

Emily looked at her. Her giddiness was adorable. "Well, good, let's beat them again then."

"Although, of course, it's not just about winning," Hailey reminded her.

Emily laughed. "Correct. It's about having fun and really enjoying another ten-hour bus ride to Valley."

After school, Emily stopped into Marget's Grocery for some frightfully expensive kitty litter. The store was mostly deserted, and she saw Jane Crockett alone in the produce section. Her first instinct was to give her a wide berth, but she overrode that.

"Hi, Mrs. Crockett," she said, setting her heavy acquisition down at her feet.

Jane looked up at her, but only briefly. "Hi," she said, giving the avocadoes her full attention.

"I don't know what the right thing to say in this situation is, but I just wanted you to know that I am very fond of both your children, and I am—"

"You'd be the first teacher," Jane said.

"I'm sorry?"

"You'd be the first teacher to be fond of my kids."

"I don't think that's true. Your kids are brilliant, well-spoken, and funny. I adore them both."

Jane looked at her then. "Well, then ... thank you."

"And I'm just sick over the Duke situation. I'm so sorry. Please let me know if there's anything I—"

"I didn't tell him to do it, you know."

"I know," Emily said, though she hadn't until that moment.

"Everyone thinks I did. As if I would put my son in harm's way like that. I did no such thing." She leaned forward onto her cart and looked at the ceiling, as if trying to persuade gravity to stop the tears from falling out of her eyes. "Oh sure, I think he did it *for* me, but I didn't want it. He was just trying to be an activist like his mama." One tear escaped and slid down her cheek. She looked at Emily. "So I'm all done anyway."

Emily didn't know what she meant, but she nodded, trying to look empathic.

"I'm done with this windmill cause. I can't win—*we* can't win anyway. The deal is already done. They're saying the windmills will be operational by the end of September. Hard to believe things can change that fast, isn't it?"

Emily nodded. "Have you heard from Duke? Is he OK?"

"No, he's terrified. He's still a little boy, you know, even though he talks big. He's not even close to OK."

"Well, like I said, I'd like to help. If there's a way to write to him, or go visit him, please let me know."

Jane looked surprised. "OK."

"OK then. You try to take care." Emily turned to go.

"My daughter really loves softball."

Emily turned back toward Jane. "That's good, because softball really loves her."

Jane smiled through her tears. "Never saw that coming. We're not much of a sports family."

"You don't have to be," Emily said.

Chapter 47

The junior class had transformed the gym/cafeteria into An Evening in Paris, complete with a black cardboard Eiffel Tower, which was listing a little to starboard, but Emily didn't want to be a critic. The gym was strung with copious strings of Christmas lights, making the space a little too well-lit to be romantic. There was glitter all over the floor, a snack table with requisite punch bowl, and a DJ playing horrible music too loud.

Emily had labored over what to wear: dressy enough to be respectful of the occasion, but not so dressy that she looked ridiculous. In the end, she was glad she had dressed down, as James was wearing what he wore to church: long-sleeved, plaid dress shirt tucked into dark jeans, and work boots. He looked scrumptious, but Emily thought she might be partial.

Emily was surprised to see the sheriff and Mr. Hogan at the door, and asked Kyle, "Are they checking for alcohol?"

"That, and many other things. Mostly just making sure no adults come in."

"What?"

"Yeah, in years past, girls have brought dates that were just a little too hairy, and we also get parents who want to come in 'just to watch,' but then end up standing around all night being creepy and ruining their kids' evenings. So that's why people have to sign any non-student guests in at the office before today, and then Mr. Hogan makes sure no one else gets in."

"That seems very strange," Emily said because she didn't know what else to say.

"I guarantee he's had to turn some parents away tonight," Kyle said. "They say they just want to take pictures, but what kid wants to dance in front of their mother?"

The small gym was filling up quickly. Sydney's dress didn't look any more expensive than anyone else's, though her hairdo, which was piled a foot on top of her head, must have cost a bit. Hailey looked gorgeous in a fitted red dress with her usually straight hair down in flowing loose curls. The Vinalhaven beau on her arm was also very handsome. But when Chloe and Thomas walked in, Emily thought her heart would burst with affection. Thomas in a tux! Chloe wore a floor-length shiny emerald green dress that showed just a bit too much skin in Emily's opinion, but she looked gorgeous. Perhaps the biggest transformation was MacKenzie— MacKenzie, whose freckled face never wore makeup wore enough that night to obscure her freckles completely. Her hair was also done up in a complex system of sparkles and braids. She looked meant-to-be on Noah's tuxedoed arm, her royal blue dress complemented by the blue pocket square on Noah's chest. It was hard to believe that girl had spent most of her spring rolling around in the dirt.

"They grow up so fast," James said in falsetto, making fun of Emily's shaky emotional state.

She elbowed him playfully. "Stop it. It *is* hard for me to see them all like this. I get so attached. I mean, they're going to graduate soon, and then what am I going to.do? How do I teach without Thomas?"

He put his arm around her and pulled her to his side. "You find another Thomas, and you love on that kid."

She looked up into his downturned face. "There's only one Thomas."

"All right then. Maybe you stay home and be a mom. No one says you have to teach."

She sighed. "Maybe. But I really love teaching."

"Speaking of babies, have you given any thought to a wedding date?" She didn't answer, because she was thinking, but her silence apparently made James nervous. "No rush, I was just curious. Totally up to you. Was just wondering if we were going to try for this summer, or if you were thinking long-term."

All of a sudden Emily was overcome with a desire to marry James, and would've done it right then and there if she could've. A flight to Vegas flashed through her mind. "I'm sorry, James. I hate that I've been paying more attention to softball than to wedding plans. Please don't read more into that than is there. I just really don't multitask well."

"You're a teacher, so I know you can multitask, but don't worry, I'm not offended. I was just curious where your thoughts were."

"My thoughts are that … wanna go to Vegas?"

He laughed. "You mean to get hitched?"

"Why else would I go to Vegas? I'm too poor to gamble."

"No, I don't want to go to Vegas. You live in the most beautiful place on earth. Don't you want to get married there?" He stopped, but then hastily added, "Unless you want to get married in your hometown. That's OK too."

"Actually, I *have* analyzed that part, and I don't want to get married in Plainfield. I think my family would rather have an excuse to come here, and then I could share this part of my life with them. Besides, I don't plan on inviting too many people. Are you OK with a small wedding?"

"Yes, just as long as it's not Vegas-chapel-small."

She giggled. "OK then. How about this summer?"

He raised an eyebrow. "Are you sure? That doesn't give us much time to plan."

"How much planning can there be? I find a dress. We find food. That's it, right?"

"Well, we need to find a place to get actually *get* married. Did you want to do it in Abe's basement?"

At first, that sounded absurd, but as she thought about it, the idea grew on her. "Maybe? You think he'd mind?"

James laughed loudly. "I don't know, but I don't think we should do that to him."

"Let's just get married outside. I could be a barefoot bride, with my toes in the ocean."

"OK, let's do it. I know just the spot."

WINDMILLS

"Bacon Poop Point?" she guessed.
"How'd you know?"

Chapter 48

On June 8, the Piercehaven Panthers softball team boarded the mid-morning ferry. As they did so, dozens of islanders cheered them on and waved signs from shore. Emily heard the cowbell, though she couldn't tell where it was coming from. It wasn't quite the same turnout that a basketball tournament ferry got, but it was close.

The ferry itself was filled to capacity with vehicles, people, and several softball-loving dogs, and Emily knew some parents (and dogs) had already taken the earlier ferry. It seemed the only islander missing was Jasmine. Apparently she was extending her own suspension. This was sad, but not heartbreaking. The girls didn't even seem to notice she was missing. They were hyper, and talking about anything *but* softball.

Emily sat down beside Juniper, who was silent. "Nervous?"

Juniper looked pensive. "I am nervous. And I'm annoyed at how nervous I am. I shouldn't be this nervous."

"It's OK to care, Juniper."

"I know. But I shouldn't be nervous. But this is the playoffs, and I feel like everybody back home is watching me."

"Did Mattawooptock make the playoffs?"

"Of course."

"Do you wish you were playing for them right now?"

Juniper looked at her.

"It's OK if you do. I can imagine you miss your friends, your home, your coach."

"I do miss all that, but no, I don't wish I was playing for them. I wouldn't be pitching, first of all, and there'd be *way* more pressure." She chewed on her lip. "Actually, you're right. I guess it could be much worse. I'm not so nervous now."

Emily wasn't nervous either, until she saw the Valley crowd. The fans had come out for both sides, making Emily suddenly feel like she was in a fishbowl at a crowded party full of fish-lovers. Before that moment, she'd felt zen about the whole thing. They had made the playoffs. They had exceeded everyone's expectations. They might win. They might lose. Either way, it would be a good thing. But now with everyone staring at her and her girls, she thought they should probably win.

She thought, too late, to ask James to coach first base. But even before she'd finished the question, she noticed he was wearing jeans.

He sighed. "Go ahead. Ask Jasper. I know you want to."

"Really? You don't think it would get me into too much trouble with the island?"

"I don't know. Right now I think they care more about winning this game than they do the windmills. Follow your gut. If you think he can help you, then ask him."

Jake Jasper, wearing snazzy red windpants, was thrilled to help.

Valley had the higher seed, so were the home team, so were in the field first. Emily called her girls together. "You hit this pitcher before. You can hit her again. Just relax. Try to ignore the crowds—and the cowbell—and just try to have fun. Be like Hannah—enjoy hitting things."

They laughed, shouted "Panthers!" and filed into the dugout. On her way by, Sara said to Emily, "My mom's here."

"Great!"

"No, you don't understand. I can't *believe* she's here. Thanks for saying what you said about me to her."

Emily gave her a small smile. The moment seemed too grave for a big one. "You're quite welcome. I just spoke the truth."

The infield collapsed on MacKenzie, making a lead-off bunt unwise. MacKenzie swung the bat instead, and struck out. They were off to a rough offensive start. Fortunately for the Panthers, the Valley girls still weren't confident batting against Juniper. So at the end of the fifth, the game was still scoreless.

Then Sara sparked a rally. It was just a little shot past the shortstop, an error really, but Valley infielders didn't make many errors, and this fired up the Piercehaven troops. Sara stood on first, her eyes scanning the Piercehaven crowd, Emily assumed, in an effort to find her mother.

"Get ready to run," Emily hollered at Sara, trying to reel her head into the game. Emily was greatly encouraged by the play, but she knew it was a long way till the top of their lineup. They were looking at seven, eight, and nine right now. "Here we go, Chloe. Keep your head down and your eye on the ball." Emily had said the words so often, she was sure they'd lost their meaning. But she didn't know what else to tell this child—this child who struggled to hit the ball off a tee. But today, Chloe squeezed her eyes shut, swung the bat, and hit the ball to shortstop for what looked to be a double play. But little Sara had a head start, and somehow, beat the ball to second base, her presence throwing the second baseman off balance as she tried to throw to first. The throw went high, and Chloe was safe. Valley had made two errors in a row. *I don't care how we get there, as long as we get there.*

Little Lucy was up and it appeared she wanted to be anywhere else. "Lucy, look at me!"

Lucy looked.

"Take a breath. You're going to be fine. Just do the best you can."

Lucy struck out.

"That's OK, Luce! It's OK!" Emily tried, but Lucy was already crying in the dugout. Allie stepped up to bat. "Hit the ball, Allie," Emily said, and then left her, and the base runners, to go see Lucy. "Lucy, look at me," she said, her tone conveying urgency. Lucy looked. "I don't want you ever crying over softball. Or any game. Do you hear me? It's just a game." Lucy sniffed and nodded, wiping at her eyes. "Good girl."

Allie hit the ball. Right at first base. But she advanced the runners. Two outs, two runners on, and a girl who thought all she could do was bunt up to bat. MacKenzie looked at Emily. Emily shook her head. *No*. MacKenzie took a deep breath and stepped into the box. And singled to right field, driving in two runs. Jake Jasper sent her to second, which scared Emily half to death, but she beat out the throw. He'd been right.

Juniper stepped up to bat looking downright cocky in her pinstripes.

"A lot can happen with two outs, Juniper," Emily said.

"I know," Juniper said, with an uncharacteristic smile.

She fouled off the first two pitches, pulling too hard.

"Wait for it to get there," Emily said.

Juniper nodded, waited, and then crack— the ball was on its way to center field. It looked like the centerfielder might get to it, but she wasn't Sara, and she couldn't quite get there before it hit the ground. MacKenzie rounded third and headed for home.

The Panthers scored five runs that inning.

Valley got one hit in the sixth and one in the seventh, but both girls were left standing on base. The Piercehaven Panthers were victorious. They were moving on to the semifinals. Hailey picked Juniper up and spun her around, with Juniper protesting the whole while. Everyone was smiling. Even DeAnna. Even Sara.

Chapter 49

The morning headline read, "Piercehaven out of nowhere." The first line read, "No one expected the Piercehaven softball team to make the playoffs, let alone advance to the semifinals." The article praised Juniper sonorously, and Emily was glad to see the reporter didn't mention that Juniper was new to the island, or how she had ended up there. The article just acted as though she was the same as any other islander. Emily wasn't proud of this train of thought, but she didn't want anyone to read the article, or hear about the game, and think, "They only won because a real pitcher moved to town." The article ended with "#6 Piercehaven (9-5) will face #2 Richmond (13-2) at Richmond on Saturday at 2."

Just the thought of it made Emily queasy. It had been bad enough playing Richmond at home. Now they had to go to Richmond. Emily closed her eyes and pictured a Maine map, trying to locate Richmond. Just south of Augusta, she thought. *Still, better get some Dramamine.*

Thanks to the medication, and lack of sleep the night before, Emily was very sleepy when the bus pulled into the Richmond High School parking lot. Emily looked out the window and couldn't believe how many familiar faces she saw. *This island really cares about its kids.* And then right on the tail of that thought, a Robert Wilson Lynd quotation came to mind: *It is in games that many men discover their paradise.*

A roar of cheers and a strong breeze greeted her as she stepped off the bus, and one or the other or both woke her up—her and her nerves. She wasn't nervous about her girls—she knew they'd do fine. She was nervous because she also knew that, barring a miracle, they were going to lose to Richmond, and she was worried about how the island would react to that. They weren't used to losing, and she didn't think they understood just how good Richmond was. How they'd only lost to Buckfield all year, and how both those games had been squeakers.

Richmond's field was heavily decorated with streamers, signs, balloons, and lots and lots of fans: maroon and white as far as the eye could see. A person—judging from their energy level, a preteen or teenaged boy—was dressed in a bobcat suit and doing cartwheels between high fives. The Richmond girls wore new, stylish uniforms and chunky maroon bows in their hair. They all wore eye black and matching face masks. Half of Emily's girls didn't even have face masks. "All right girls, take a lap," she said, trying to get herself out of her own head.

Jake Jasper approached. "Hi, Coach!"

She tried to return his chipper tone. "Hey!"

He smiled as if to say he knew she was faking. "What do you think?"

"Honestly? I think we're going to get killed."

He chuckled, rubbing his stubbled chin. "Yeah, that's a possibility."

After a quick warmup, the umps called for coaches and captains. Emily invited Jake to join them in the pre-game conference. Then she called for her captains. "Ava, MacKenzie, Hailey, and Juniper, come on!" Hailey looked surprised, but Juniper looked shocked.

The conference was a study in pleasantries. It seemed to take forever to get all the hands shook.

After the conference, Emily called the girls in for a last second huddle, and tried to inject confidence in her voice. "All right, ladies. This is a great moment for us. We are in the big leagues now, but we aren't here by accident. We've earned the right to be here. So let's do the best we can and have some fun. This pitcher's good, and she's not going to walk very many, if any, of you. So we're going to have to be hitters, but that's not a problem. You've hit this girl before, and you can hit her today. OK? Confidence! Believe in one another. Believe in yourselves. Ready? Here we go. Bring it in."

MacKenzie led off with a left-handed bunt and was promptly thrown out. The play was close, but the ball beat her there. The Piercehaven fans thought otherwise, however, and began to harass the umpire. *Oh no, please don't turn them against us.*

Juniper grounded out. Then Ava struck out. After she did so, she looked at the bat in her hands as if it were a foreign object and she didn't know quite what it was or how it got there.

Richmond got their first three batters on, then scored a run, and then struck out three times in a row. "Thanks for getting us out of that one, Juniper."

She nodded sternly.

"OK, ladies, they only got one run. We can get that back. Here we go!"

WINDMILLS

"Hannah, Hailey, Sara," Thomas called out the lineup.

Hannah arrived at the plate as if she was born to be there. Then she singled to right field. Hailey struck out. Sara struck out. Chloe struck out. Poor Hannah trudged off first base.

The second inning was scoreless.

Lucy led off at the top of the third. She struck out, but the catcher missed the catch. Jake hollered at her to run, and she did. Piercehaven had a runner on. Allie stepped up, looking terrified. She took the first pitch, which was a strike. She took the second pitch, which was a strike. Emily resisted the urge to scream at her to swing the bat. "Protect the plate, Allie," Emily said instead. Allie took the third strike, which was a change-up, and sure looked like a strike from where Emily stood, but the ump called it a ball. "Protect the plate," Emily repeated, trying to sound encouraging. Allie swung at the fourth pitch and fouled it off. Then she fouled off the fifth pitch. And then she fouled off the sixth, seventh, and eighth pitch. *This is turning into the longest at bat in history.* Emily felt sympathy for the pitcher. Allie took the ninth pitch, and it appeared to be right down the middle. Emily's heart sank. But the ump sent Allie to first. *Rallies have started with less.*

MacKenzie stepped up and looked to Emily for the bunt sign. Emily shook her head. MacKenzie looked disappointed, but she didn't argue. She swung the bat with all her might, just grazed the top of the ball, and the ball rolled toward the pitcher with an embarrassing lack of oomph. MacKenzie took off. The pitcher turned and threw Lucy out at third. Emily tried to hide her disappointment, but she wasn't disappointed for long, because Juniper stepped up and cracked a single to right, and Emily sent Allie home. It was a tied game.

Ava stepped up to bat and hit the ball right to the second baseman, who looked MacKenzie back to third, and then easily threw Ava out at first. Two outs, two talented ducks on the pond, and Emily's cleanup batter was up. Hannah swung at the first pitch and drove it into deep left.

"Run!" Emily screamed.

"Run!" Jake Jasper shouted.

"Run!" every citizen of Piercehaven yelled.

The girls ran as the ball soared and soared; with no sign of slowing down, it soared all the way over the fence—and about three inches to the left of the pole that marked the terminus of the third base line. Half the Piercehaven crowd fell silent, but that noise vacuum was instantly filled with a hundred Richmonders loudly pointing out what the umpires had so obviously seen. The ump behind the plate held his arms up as high as they would go. "Foul ball! Foul fall! Runners return to base!"

It took some time to calm everyone down and fill everyone in. Hannah was particularly hard to convince, as if by refusing to accept it, she could move her hit four inches to the right and make it fair. She finally, grudgingly picked the bat up again. Then she tried to crush the ball, and popped up to third base, where it was caught with ease.

The score remained 1 to 1.

Juniper was pitching the game of her life. But in the bottom of the fifth, the Bobcats hit back-to-back singles. The next girl hit a double, and just like that, the score was 3 to 1. The Richmond crowd went nuts. Emily silently thanked God they didn't have a cowbell. But Richmond wasn't done. Another single, an error, and a long shot to right drove in three more runs.

The proverbial wind had been ripped out of Piercehaven's sails.

The top of the sixth registered three quick K's for the Panthers. Emily put some subs in.

The bottom of the sixth garnered one more run for the Bobcats.

Before the top of the seventh, Emily called the girls together. MacKenzie and Hannah were already crying. "Listen to me," Emily said, and could tell most of them were not listening at all. "Listen to me," she said more sharply. Most of them snapped to attention. "It's OK to be disappointed, but I don't want anyone crying over softball. This is a *game*. And this might be our last inning for the season, so let's try to have some fun. You have a choice—go home with your heads hanging or your chins held high—it's up to you."

"Sara, DeAnna, and Natalie," Thomas called out the lineup.

Sara stepped up to bat.

Sara struck out.

Emily praised her efforts, and then turned her attention and encouragement to DeAnna.

DeAnna certainly didn't look the part. She was probably the only softball player in the state playing in a semifinal game with her hair down. It spilled out the back of her helmet, making her already non-athletic, gangly batting stance look all the more singular. But DeAnna swung the bat, and that's what Piercehaven needed, much more than they needed her to look the part. She hit the ball up the first base line. It rolled foul, but the first baseman didn't pick it up in time, and it rolled fair as DeAnna crossed over first base. The Richmond coach was not pleased.

Up stepped senior Natalie. Emily knew there were at least a dozen Greems there cheering her on; she'd seen them, and now she could hear them. Natalie didn't have much game experience, and she hadn't shown much potential. Emily didn't have a lot of hope.

But Natalie made contact, and the ball rolled pitifully toward third. The third baseman expertly picked the ball up and fired it to first, getting the second out. But Natalie had moved DeAnna over.

It was time for Sydney Hopkins to step up. Emily closed her eyes and took a breath, in an effort to calm her own emotional maelstrom. *This is only a game*. Her eyes popped open at the definitive sound of bat on ball. Sydney had ripped one up the middle, and here came DeAnna, her eyes wild, begging for instruction, her crazy hair flowing straight out behind her, riding her wake. Emily began waving her home. "You're going to have to slide. Wheels, DeAnna, wheels!" It turned out DeAnna didn't have to slide, but she did anyway.

The crowd went nuts. Emily could hear PeeWee spewing accolades for his daughter, and was only moderately annoyed.

ROBIN MERRILL

It was 7 to 2. Two outs. And the Panthers were at the top of their lineup.

Chapter 50

They needed five runs. It would take a miracle. Stranger things had happened.

Sydney stood on first base.

MacKenzie looked at Emily, her eyes begging for the bunt. Emily shook her head. "Hit the ball, kiddo. You are long overdue."

MacKenzie looked skeptical. She tried to work the pitcher, even faking a bunt once, but all she did was work herself into a full count.

"Got to protect now," Emily said.

Emily would never know if what happened next was intentional on MacKenzie's part. MacKenzie would deny it adamantly, but it was just a little too poetic to have been coincidence. MacKenzie swung at the next pitch, and as she did so, the pitch caught her in the left shoulder. She cried out. It was believable that a girl would cry out when hit by a pitch traveling that fast. It was less believable that MacKenzie would. The umpire sent her to first base, which she took, holding her left shoulder. It was the last time she would exhibit any pain from that injury.

Juniper was up to bat, and Emily's heart swelled with affection for her. It was hard to believe what a row they'd had less than two months before. Juniper belted the ball right to the pitcher, who managed to slow it down with her glove, but all that accomplished was making it harder for the shortstop to get to it. The third baseman charged the ball as well, leaving third base uncovered. The left fielder came to cover, but Sydney beat her there.

Emily thought she might be having a heart attack.

Ava missed the first two strikes, fouled off a change-up, and then singled the next pitch up the middle.

The scoreboard changed to 7 to 3. They were playing in the weeds, but they were still playing.

Hannah stepped up to bat smiling.

Lord, please don't let her get cocky.

She grounded into centerfield. Everyone advanced one base. 7 to 4.

Hailey stepped up to the plate. She too gave Emily a few gray hairs waiting till the third strike before swinging the bat, but she finally did swing, and sent the ball between first and second, sending Juniper home: 7 to 5.

WINDMILLS

The Richmond coach was pulling his hair out. The Richmond pitcher looked worried. The fans were on their feet.

It was Sara's turn. She swung at the first pitch—and missed. She swung at the second—and fouled it off. The third pitch was a change-up, and threw Sara off balance. Still, she swung—and completely missed the ball. And that was it. The inning was over. The game was over. The season was over. Sara collapsed. She fell to her knees in the batter's box and bent over home plate as if praying. Her shoulders shook with sobs—sobs no one could hear over Richmond's celebration.

Emily started toward Sara but then stopped. Because Juniper was already there. Juniper reached down and took one of Sara's hands and gently pulled her to her feet. Then she undid Sara's chinstrap and lifted the batting helmet off Sara's head. She tossed the helmet toward the dugout and then wrapped her arms around Sara's small frame; Sara rested her head on Juniper's shoulder as the team gathered around them both. Hailey put her arms around them from one side, MacKenzie from the other. Hannah joined the embrace, then Chloe, then the rest. DeAnna came too. And though she didn't touch anyone, she did stand close enough to be a part of the large, silent huddle—a huddle that centered on the girl whose brother had threatened to blow up the windmills and the girl whose dad was building them.

Emily, tears rolling down her cheeks, thought, *This couldn't get any more beautiful.* But she was wrong. Because MacKenzie's mom joined the hug. Then Chloe's mom. Chloe left the pack then, ran to the dugout, grabbed Thomas's hand, and led him back to the team. By then, Hannah's mom had joined the group. Then Ava's grandmother put one arm around DeAnna and drew her into the fold. Then the entire Greem family joined in. Then Jane Crockett, her dreads held up with a bright red scarf and her cheeks shiny with tears. Most of the fans had left their folding chairs and were joining in the embrace. Even PeeWee Hopkins stood uncomfortably on the outside, with one hand on Hailey's dad's shoulder.

As the Richmond crowd dispersed, Jake Jasper approached Emily from behind. "That's quite an island you've got there," he said.

Emily took a deep breath of spring air. "Yeah. We have our moments."

Epilogue

On Monday morning, Thomas's stepmom, school board member Abby Payne, came to see Emily at school. "Just wanted to say thank you for what you did this spring, with the girls. Also wanted to let you know that the school board has every intention of having a softball team next year, and for years to come. Of course, there's no pressure, but if you're willing to coach again, the job is yours. And we'll even pay you this time."

"Thank you," Emily said. "Can we also get new uniforms? The girls hate pinstripes."

* * *

Large Print Books by Robin Merrill

Piercehaven Trilogy
Piercehaven
Windmills
Trespass

New Beginnings
Knocking
Kicking
Searching

Shelter Trilogy
Shelter
Daniel
Revival

Wing and a Prayer Mysteries
The Whistle Blower
The Showstopper
The Pinch Runner
The Prima Donna

Gertrude, Gumshoe Cozy Mystery Series
Introducing Gertrude, Gumshoe
Gertrude, Gumshoe: Murder at Goodwill
Gertrude, Gumshoe and the VardSale Villain
Gertrude, Gumshoe: Slam Is Murder
Gertrude, Gumshoe: Gunslinger City
Gertrude, Gumshoe and the Clearwater Curse

Want the inside scoop?
Visit robinmerrill.com to join
Robin's Readers!

*Robin also writes sweet romance
as Penelope Spark:*

Sweet Country Music Romance
The Rising Star's Fake Girlfriend
The Diva's Bodyguard
The Songwriter's Rival

Clean Billionaire Romance
The Billionaire's Cure
The Billionaire's Secret Shoes
The Billionaire's Blizzard
The Billionaire's Chauffeuress
The Billionaire's Christmas

Manufactured by Amazon.ca
Bolton, ON